Nicety

Presents

Juicy

Pandora's Box

A Novel

Find out more about the author and upcoming novels online at
Facebook: https://www.facebook.com/ NicetyCouture
Twitter: @NicetyCouture

ACKNOWLEDGMENTS

Thank you to my family, I will love you all until the end of time. You are the air that I breathe. To my friends, thanks for keeping me afloat when I thought I would sink. To my cover model, Siobhon "Lovesem" Georgy, thanks for doing your thing on the photos. You rock everyday! To my fans and many followers, I love you all more and more each day. Thank you for the love and support you deliver each day!

To book Siobhon "Lovesem" Georgy for cover modeling contact lovesem.true@gmail.com

DEDICATION

I would like to dedicate this book to my family and my friends who supported me and my dream of becoming a published writer. They believed in me when I didn't believe in myself years ago. I'm making you proud now! Also to my readers for without you there would be no me. I love you all!

To some very special readers who have been rocking with me and supporting me from day one, I love you all. Thanks to Latosha Scruggs, Jackie Figueroa, Yung-Lit, Tiffany Haynes, Camille Lamb, Nefertaria Ayo, Fallon Willis Blaqk, Keyanna Savage, Shemika Jones and Tanisha-PhatPhat.

To my besties…you all know who you are as I will only use first names but your love and support knows no bounds. Mario, Guillermo, Ashley H., Ashley P., and Ashley P. (Yes I meant to do that), Jeanne, Yvette, Bob, Manny "You're so silly",

Arndell, Leslie, Princess, Walt, Aisha, Will, Karen, Theresa, Candice, Tiffany K., Irine, Meron, Earline and Jermika. I want to thank you from the bottom of my heart for always supporting me and making sure that I stayed focused on the task at hand. To my husband, your love is like a wondrous dream that I never want to awake from. I love you, babe!

If I have forgotten anyone, know that I love you still.

More Titles from Nicety
Available on Kindle & Nook

 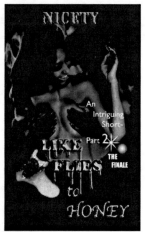

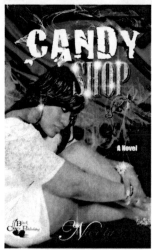

(Candy Shop is available in paperback as well)

"Live your life like it's golden. For tomorrow is never promised today."
Nicety

Chapter 1- Fed Up

Her pussy throbbed as hard as her heart thumped. The heavy panting she released made her dizzy and light headed. She ran her fingers up across her full breasts then down in between her vivacious legs. Two fingers slipped effortlessly into her slit as she moaned softly, loving the penetration feeling moving inside of her. Her legs were cocked up in the air, pointing straight as if she was a ballerina and then they retracted as she began to tremble.

"Give it to me baby. Yes! Yes!" She exclaimed needing, desiring more.

She licked her index and middle fingers on her free hand leaving them nicely moist and dripping with saliva then moved them down to her clitoris rubbing it profusely and forcing it to become erect. Her other hand forced the penetration harder and harder as she struggled to cum in a haste. Time was running out, if she didn't burst now she would never do it. She moaned wildly hoping to help the cum release but it was no use. It was too late and the timer had buzzed. It was all over. She looked down at her failed pussy and began slapping it.

"Fuck!"

Pandora awoke on the couch in a dripping hot sweat. She looked around realizing that it was all merely a dream. Not only was she still at home but she was also still alone and still a virgin. *I'm tired of being the goody two shoes. I need some dick dammit.* She thought as she slammed her hands against the couch and stomped her feet in an angry temper tantrum. Her head began spinning becoming lightheaded as she tried to calm down and rose turning on her Bose stereo then cranking the volume up as high as it would go.

"She ain't fucking with you 'less you got a lot o' money..."

Power 92 blared throughout the Beverly area home and Diamond's Lotta Money prompted Pandora to bob her head and sing along. It was the summer anthem and everybody seemed to be listening to the same station as it blared through her open windows as well. She looked at the clock on the Comcast cable box realizing she didn't have much time left. The house was usually spotless on a daily basis but for some reason her father wanted it to be immaculate everyday. Before he checked anything else he checked the dust content like clockwork on the mantle first. It was where her beautiful mother Vivian sat. Her urn sat below her life size picture, which adorned the wall above.

Pandora dusted carefully around the urn making sure to clean without so much as tipping it and along the rest of the mantle. She then pressed two fingertips against her full lips for a kiss and smacked them against the bottom of her mother's picture.

"Love you, ma." She said as she grabbed the broom from it's lean on the wall and began to continue her chores.

****

Vivian was a beautiful exotic, Jamaican beauty queen and model. She grew up an orphan in Jamaica but at sixteen fled to the states with some of her friends as stow-a-ways on a liquor boat. They were so frail from malnutrition that no one even saw them hiding behind the small wooden barrels in the back. When they reached America, they all split up wanting to enjoy the freedom the states had to offer without added baggage.

For the first few years, she lived on the streets wearing tattered clothes and shoes, which she often stole from the back of thrift stores and ate scraps other people didn't want from restaurant tables. She lucked up on a job working in a sweat factory from a truck driver she was about to rob. He had a friend who hooked her up so she ended up staying in Miami instead of venturing to New York as she had originally planned. She wanted to be a contemporary dancer but all of that flew out if the window when she ended up working two years for chump change. The day Vivian was discovered by a modeling agent changed her world.

"Hey girly. Your face is really pretty." The older woman said smoking on her cigarette and sipping her latte.

"Eh, tell me something I don't know." Vivian replied having heard it all before.

"What would you say if I told you I could make you a star?" The woman snarled not impressed by Vivian's cockiness.

"I would say get lost bitch." Vivian replied rolling her eyes and walking past the woman butting shoulders.

She was a very sassy smart aleck young woman and being on her own forced her to have her guard up all the time. Men and women tried her at every given moment but she was very high-strung and wasn't having any of it. Vivian carried a box cutter with her at all times that she had found in a dumpster when she first began working. If she needed to fight to the death, she did what it took to save her ass.

"Here's my card."

The woman handed her card over with jittery hands from Vivian's words. She wanted to sign the next hottest thing with high cheekbones, curvy hips, and mellifluous skin but she didn't know she was getting a feisty bullfighter. "Call me tomorrow. If you're interested, you could come by the office and we'll get you started."

"We'll see." Vivian played it cool. She didn't want to seem too anxious just in case the woman was real and she needed to negotiate a huge deal.

She had to admit that being approached with an opportunity of a lifetime like that excited her. Seeing her face on the cover of a magazine that would be on sale around the world or ripping the runway, would have been her greatest accomplishment ever, since leaving her homeland. The next day, Vivian signed a six-figure deal with Elite Model Management and the rest was history.

****

Pandora quickly swept the very little trash of dust underneath the couch and tucked the broom and dustpan away in the pantry. She looked around making sure nothing was out of place and everything was spotless. The dishes were cleaned, dried and placed in the cabinet. The throw pillows were straightened on both leather sofas and the trash was taken out. The jiggle of keys and the doorknob at the front door startled her as she stood in the middle of the hallway with her head down and arms crossed behind her back. She patiently waited on the figure to emerge from around the corner of the wall and as soon as it did her heart dropped.

"Hello Pastor." Pandora said never once looking up into his eyes.

"Are the chores done?" He asked as he looked directly at the mantle where the remains of his wife sat.

The pastor wasn't really a pastor at all. He had recently been practicing to become one at their church on 76th and Halsted. He hadn't been ordained yet but he demanded that people addressed him as such anyway. It was one of his many hustles. Vivian met him on location one day when she was shooting a spread for a magazine. Then he was a production assistant and was too cute for words with his long dark curly hair and his baby face. He always wore white tees and jeans giving him this thug-like appearance, which drew Vivian in immediately. His persona intrigued her along with his chestnut eyes and small nerd-like physique. He was perfect in every way to her.

Soon after they began to fool around she became pregnant with the twins but they never married leaving him frustrated and penniless when she died. She had paid for the house before she died but the upkeep of it was breaking him. Now he was a skinny beer bellied, gray haired 42-year-old drunk who had financial problems, worked odd jobs to get by and sought becoming a pastor as an answer to his prayers. He felt the church would take care of all of his needs and expenses and it would be a cakewalk to get the funds he needed to stay afloat.

"Yes, sir." Pandora answered hoping everything was to his liking.

The pastor walked and began inspecting further rubbing his finger across the kitchen countertops and checking the refrigerator for one thing moved out of place. Then he returned back to the living room and made sure the flowers on the urn were turned towards the sun just like he liked it. Vivian loved the way painted glass looked in the sunlight so he had a stained glass window installed so he could keep her urn facing flowers out towards it.

"Very good, Pandora. Very good." He said plopping down on the sofa dropping his workbag on the floor like it was nothing. He kicked off his worn black work shoes then used his toes to pry his sticky wet socks off of his humongous feet. He then kicked them to the side like they were garbage, leaving the stench of hot garbage to fester in the room. "Where are your sisters?"

"They are still at the grocery store picking up the items on shopping list." Pandora lied covering her nose.

They had already brought the food home and had left back out to watch the ballers play basketball at the court up the street. They weren't watching for the game, though, they were watching for the sexy bodies and flashy cars those niggas stunted in. The neighborhood dudes their age were too young minded and never had money to spend but the high rollers didn't care about spending money. Diamond was seasoned in the game and now she was putting Lexi up on it since her twin was somewhat of a prude.

Pandora was amazed the pastor hadn't seen them on his walk home from the bus stop since the park was directly across the street from it. They knew what he would do if he caught them but they always took that risk in order to do what they wanted. Pandora didn't like the fact that her identical twin, Diamond, was twenty four minutes older than her but she wasn't the one playing the big sister. She wanted her to be more responsible around the house to take some of the burden off of her but her rebellious side took over and was rubbing off on their younger sister Lexi really fast.

Lexi was only 2 years younger than them but she was a pistol. She was hot headed just like their mother and didn't take shit from no one. It was a hard subject for all of them to talk about but their mother died struggling for fourteen hours trying to bring Lexi into the world. She was able to give her one smile then collapsed on the delivery table. Doctors revived her and she remained brain dead for two weeks before their father decided to give up and cut the life support. It was hard for him to let go as well so he had her cremated and began drinking to keep his sanity.

The girls were the spitting images of their Jamaican roots with their honey brown skin and high cheekbones. The twins had long dark hair with golden brown eyes and bodies made like goddesses. They stood about 5'3" and were known as the "lil bits" of the neighborhood. It was weird to them how they scarfed down everything in sight but never gained a pound. The bulk of it went inside of their pants to their thick waists while the rest ended up in their 32C cups.

Lexi, though still a teenager, was busting out all over like she was fresh out of a hip-hop music video. She was slightly taller than them standing 5'5" but she wore flats so she could look shorter. The attention her sisters got for being short made her want to be recognized for the same cuteness. She had ass for days and a D cup rack that made grown men stop to drool. Her hair was long but she cut it into a layered bob once she got wind of Toya's bob on BET. With her angelic face and thick dark makeup, it fit her perfectly.

"Get me a beer then get in here and read the word with me." The pastor demanded.

Pandora rolled her eyes and smacked her lips as she trotted towards the kitchen snatching the ice cold Bud out the refrigerator. She was tired of listening to his wannabe gospel scriptures, everybody was. He would always open the book pretending to read from it but he was actually free styling the words, which didn't make a lick of sense to her. The whole time he spoke she would only be wondering why the hell her sisters didn't have to listen to that shit. She plopped down next to him handing him the beer.

As he spoke and sipped his beer he paused gazing up at Vivian cutting a quick smile. Missing her was like missing a heartbeat, unbearable. She had been gone for so long but his yearning for her smell, her touch, her being never went away. He let out a small sigh as he took another sip of his beer and ran his fingers slowly down the front of Pandora's tied up tank top.

He reached for her right breast twirling his fingers around her nipple. Pandora became aroused and confused all at the same time. He had never touched her this way so she wasn't sure what to make of it.

"Dad, what are you doing?" Pandora asked meekly as a tingling feeling came over her.

"DAD!" The pastor yelled, snapping abruptly. "Is that what you call me, dad? I'm a pastor and you will not disrespect me."

He stood releasing the thick leather belt from his pants raising his hands straight up in the air then delivering a mighty blow right on to Pandora's legs. She screamed higher then the clouds as she dropped to the floor on her knees curling up while he ravaged her back. She balled up tightly praying for it to end but it seemed it never would.

"You will learn respect! All of you, will learn!" He spat.

"Stop! Please just stop!" Pandora yelled but her cries went unnoticed.

Her coco brown skin began to turn red as welts formed across her back. Diamond and Lexi returned home storming in the house rushing to the living room to see what she had done to make him mad. There was no question as to what he was doing since they had all been in that position many times before with the pastor. His anger superseded any good they had ever done. Nothing made him happy.

But after searching through a box of old letters her mother had marked and stored away for her right before she died, Diamond had learned the truth, and hid it from everyone else. She felt it was her mother's way of connecting with her even in death.

"Pastor, leave her alone!" Lexi screamed.

He didn't hear anything past the voice of his own rage. Lexi and Diamond both rushed him. Lexi jumped on his back and Diamond threw blows aiming for his dick but as he was fighting back she only reached his stomach. He swung Lexi's thick frame around roughly sending her flying into the mantle making the urn fall down on top of her. She sat on the floor with tears in her eyes that refused to fall and covered in Vivian's ashes. Everyone paused unable to move any further. All they could do was stare at the mess they had all created and what was left of their dearly missed mother.

"Look what the fuck you did!" Pandora screamed wildly.

She slowly crawled over to her sister trying to scrape the ashes from her skin and hair.

"It's useless. It just keeps smearing." Lexi said as she joined her sister in the cleanup effort.

The pastor stood there with not one tear in his eye glaring down at the girls. Diamond was still standing next to him giving the most devilish and most sinister look anyone could ever give. He pretended it didn't faze him as he walked by her and headed up to his room.

Diamond closed her eyes as he stammered up the stairs and slammed the door. She opened her eyes immediately after enraged at the sight before her.

"Get up! Get the fuck up!" Diamond said silently through her teeth.

"We have to save momma." Lexi whined holding her hands up so she wouldn't smear her mother on her clothes.

"No. Momma's gone and ain't shit we can do to change that. But we're too grown to be up in this house with him. It's time we left." Diamond said looking at her two sisters.

Pandora was shocked at how her sister was taking charge of the situation. Before Diamond would never lift a finger no matter who told her to do it. Her beatings came swift and easy but she took them like a vet because she refused to do anything for his ass. It was hard for anyone to believe what Diamond was saying though, since she very rarely kept her word. But the look in her eyes told the girls a different story that day.

"Di, how the fuck are we gonna leave? We don't have no money and no place to go." Pandora retorted.

"You let me take care of that. But whatever I say goes. You have to listen to me and do what I say cause if you don't we're dead for sure. So, you in?" Diamond said huddling the girls up like they were in the last quarter of the WNBA finals.

"I don't know about this, Di. Dead? I ain't trying to die, shit." Pandora said shaking her head.

"If you stay here you're a dead bitch anyway. Period."
Diamond retorted giving her a shrug.

"Well fuck that! I'm in!" Lexi said shaking up with
Diamond, ready to get it cracking on her plan.

"What's your plan Di?" Pandora rebutted.

"Bitch my plan is to get rich or die tryin'. Now are
you in or out?" Diamond started to become angry.

She wasn't one to explain her self or plead her case to
anyone no matter who they were. Furthermore, she didn't
appreciate the fact that Pandora was questioning her. It
shouldn't have mattered what her plan was just as long as it
worked so they could get the fuck out of the hellhole they
lived in.

"Fine, Di, I'm in." Pandora reluctantly agreed.

"Cool. Look, I promise I ain't gon' let nothing
happen to either of you. Y'all my blood and y'all all I got."
Diamond said giving her sisters a heartfelt group hug.

Chapter 2- The Plan

The next day Diamond and Lexi began to go to work. Pandora was to remain at the house and play everything cool as usual. It was important that nothing changed in their daily routines so when it was time for them to leave it would be swift and clean leaving no trace. They staked out the basketball court at 3pm like they did on any other day sitting atop the bleachers.

They wore their shortest jean shorts with tank tops and push up bras accentuating their youthful breasts. The brightly colored platform heels they wore elongated their lovely toned legs. The sisters scoped out the ballers and sized them up to see which one of them would become their victim. The court was like the midday kickin' it spot where fellas came to unwind from all of the stress in their lives. Some of them balled hard making wagers and tossing globs of sweat from their solid bodies all across the court. But mostly they all hung out on the bleachers chatting it up, smoking loud, and checking for banging hood rats to take home for a few hours.

Lexi huddled up with Diamond speaking low enough so that no one else could hear her. She nudged her head in the direction of the prospects she was picking out careful not to seem too obvious but everyone she was picking was not to Diamond's standards. Hard core rap music rattled the park's parking lot. The handful of cars over there all had butterfly doors on them and they were all pointed up in the air with old school candy coated paint. Diamond was impressed and began to salivate when she noticed they all had twenty two-inch rims.

"There. Over there." Diamond said pointing inconspicuously over towards the lot.

"What them? No Di, they're all ugly." Lexi retorted shaking her head in disgust.

"Girl what is you trippin' about? It ain't like we trying to marry these niggas or nothing. We just trying to get that chedda." Diamond said.

Lexi looked into her sister's eyes already knowing what her plan was. She was down for anything but with ugly niggas, that's where she drew her line. Even if she popped all the Yompers in the world it wouldn't keep her from vomiting all over an ugly ass nigga's dick. She gazed over to the lot then back at Diamond with a raised eyebrow.

"I'm just saying, do they have to be ugly?" Lexi asked.

"Bitch, I wouldn't care if they were as black as roaches. We ain't on nothing but this money." Diamond snapped.

Lexi shook her head but understood where her sister was coming from. She smacked her lips then glanced over to the men. Not one of them was appealing enough to choose in her eyes but she lifted her finger slightly pointing to one of the ones who looked like he had the most money. Diamond looked over across the field noticing one of her long time bustdowns standing with his crew in the cut. She hadn't seen him in a few days and wondered what kind of shit was he trying to pull not calling her but she was about to find out.

"Hold that thought lil' sis. I'll be right back." Diamond said never taking her eyes off of her target.

Lexi caught an attitude at Diamond because she was losing sight of the task at hand, not to mention she was always leaving her for a five minute fuck. Diamond eased across the field hoping she was being inconspicuous. She crept up behind Shug and covered his eyes with her hands smiling playfully. Shug ususally didn't like that kind of shit, not being a man to play too many games but he had already known whom it was. There was only one female who he allowed to play with him like that and that was because he had soft spot in his heart for her.

"What's good nigga? What you can't call nobody?" Diamond said coming around to face him.

"Naw girl. Shit it's only been a few days and I've just been on something lately. What's good?" Shug responded.

"Shit you what's up." She said with allure in her eyes.

"Damn we've been fucking around for three years and you can't go one day without this Daddy Dick huh?" Shug chuckled.

"Whatever nigga. Just come on." Diamond said headed for his Beamer.

Shug shook up with his dudes as they taunted him for bailing on them for a female but he didn't care. Shug was originally from Brooklyn, NY but came to Chicago for a change of scenery. He was a kind hearted yet ruthless type of dude but you couldn't tell that by looking at him. He was a 5'9", three hundred pound chocolate skinned man with a sexy baby face and love me long time dick. His shoe size was a fifteen, which drew attention from women far and wide along with the fact that his money was just as long. Even though he was a large guy he carried his self in a sexy way. He stayed clean from head to toe and was the type of dude to never rock dirt on his kicks. He also loved to give back to the hood loving to help people that weren't as fortunate as he. Growing up in poverty he knew what it felt like to struggle and even though he didn't have any kids of his own he couldn't bare to see the kids go hungry buying groceries if needed to.

Shug plopped down in the driver's seat and slammed the door. He started the car then glanced over a Diamond who looked comfortable with her polished toes kicked up on his dashboard. It amused him that she was that comfortable with him so he blew it off cause if it was anybody else he would've snapped.

He whipped the corner slowly turning off into an alley behind the block. He slowed the car down around half of the way down the alley then pulled very closely along side of one of the garages and cut the car off. In broad daylight, amongst a row of garbage cans lined up ad down the alley, Diamond unbuckled Shug's pants, pulled them down and got to work.

She slobbered up and down his shaft like she was sucking on her favorite flavor Popsicle. Every time she sucked him off it reminded her of the first time they met. Shug was one of the first niggas she had ever try to play for money but little did Diamond know he would school her with knowledge to play the dummies for a lifetime. At fifteen years old, she interrupted him in the middle of his cypher with his dudes and asked him for a ride home. She ended up giving him a ride instead then asked for a thousand dollars so she could go shopping. He gurgled liking her style and lowered the money to her just because she worked hard for it. But right before he did he let her know a very important piece of information pertaining to her game.

"Baby, you ain't got to spread ya legs to every nigga to get them to show you love ma. Ya beauty speaks for itself. Let them niggas pay for just getting a glimpse of that shit. Ya feel me?" He said.

From that day forward they were inseparable. Once she had caught his cum in her mouth, she swallowed it down and returned to her seat. She looked over at him waiting for a response but received none.

He didn't like attitudes so she knew getting one with him was out of the question. She huffed and puffed waiting for him to ask what was wrong but Shug never gave in. As he regained his composure and buckled his pants back up she knew her opportunity was slipping away from her.

"Aight, Shug. I need help." She said exhaling heavily.

"What's the deal?"

"Um, I kinda need some money."

"You kinda need some money or you do need some money?" He asked clearing his throat.

"Well, I do." Diamond said fiddling with her fingernails.

"How much Diamond?"

"Shit a lot. How much can you give me?"

I got about two stacks on me right now. So, how much you talking?" Shug rubbed his finger under his nose.

"Naw baby, I need like ten large. Just to get me started then I can make the rest. Probably find me a job or something." Diamond said.

"Huh? Most females ask for change to get their hair did or something. Shoes. What you need wit' that kind of dough shorty?"

"I need to get me and my sisters out from under my bitch ass father. His abuse is killing us. We can't take it no more. It's just to pay rent up for a minute until we can find jobs and stuff. So will you help us?" She said innocently.

"Listen baby girl. I got mad love for you and all. But I can't see myself giving you that much money and you ain't my bitch and all. I'll help you as best as I can but that shit, I'm good on."

"You good on? Nigga I've been fucking and sucking on you for years and you mean to tell me that I ain't good for it?" Diamond said embarrassed and disappointed at the same time.

"Girl you trippin'. Let me drive you back to the spot before you say something you gon' regret." Shug said revving the car back up.

"Naw nigga you trippin' wit' yo' fat ass. Gon' deny me when you out here spreading your fat ass oats to every fucking body but when somebody needs real help you play stupid. Fuck you nigga, I'll walk." Diamond snapped exiting the car.

She wanted to slam his car door so hard that the glass shattered but she knew that a man as big as he shouldn't be aggravated in that nature. Calling him names was one thing but fucking with his car was something too extreme. She headed down the alley without turning back to see if he was still there or if he had driven off. All she knew is that she could still hear his car running behind her.

"Hoes never get paid, baby girl." Shug yelled out the car window as he sped off screeching the tires for effect.

Diamond turned the corner on the alley. With the court in sight she headed back for the bleachers where Lexi was still sitting, angry yet waiting patiently. The men that they were peeping earlier were still out there chilling when she walked up the bleachers and sat down next to her sister. Lexi turned to see the distraught look on her face and automatically knew she was upset about something that happened with Shug.

"Didn't go as planned, huh?" Lexi said casually.

"Girl fuck that nigga. I'm through with him." Diamond said trying to save face.

"Mmhmm." Lexi replied squeezing her lips tightly. "So, what about him?" She asked curling up her lips.

Diamond focused her eyes in on the medium build, caramel complexioned guy leaning on the gate and smoking a blunt. His muscles were nicely defined and his fresh looking white tee made him appear so clean. Though he was a few feet away from his car, she knew he had to own one of the expensive ones. Diamond knew exactly who he was but his arrogant demeanor kept her from ever approaching him. Other chicks used to boast about how good his sex was but he treated them like they were gum on the bottom of his shoe. Nonetheless, Diamond knew that he was ripe for the picking because his money was so long he could feed the homeless of Chicago for years to come.

He wasn't about nickeling and diming with petty street figures, he only dealt in weight, something he let be known to anyone who asked to work for him. She wished she could have gotten to his connect but he was the next best thing.

"That's him, Lex. That's our victim." Diamond said licking her lips finishing with a slight smirk.

"Shit, he sure looks like he got plenty of dough." Lexi said getting a better glance at his gear. "Alright, so how do we get this fool?"

"Girl, you know how we do. We give him the pussy and put that ass to sleep and while he's snoozing, we get his ass."

"Yeah but Di, we ain't never mess with nobody like that. This ain't just a few dollars out of a nigga's wallet, D. This is straight jacking a made nigga." Lexi said.

"Okay. This will be no different, trust me. I got this all mapped out. But we need an innocent face…someone who doesn't look like any of these gold digging skanks out here cause he'll sniff her out a mile away." Diamond said placing her chin on her knuckles in thinking mode.

"Hello? Pandora, duh." Lexi said muffing Diamond in the head. "She's as innocent as they come."

Diamond shook her head in agreement as she took out a box of Newport 100s from her pocket. She took one out then placed it slowly to her luscious pink shimmer lip glossed lips and sparked it up. She nudged Lexi in the direction of the exit letting her know it was time to go. The sisters left the bleachers but Diamond pulled Lexi's arm before she headed out of the park.

"We goin' over there." Diamond said.

"For what?" Lexi retorted.

"So we can check this nigga out."

Lexi rolled her eyes but followed Diamond over to the parking lot anyway. The closer they got to the group of men the more Diamond's heart jumped. She was used to messing with low-level niggas who were all hood and easily played. They were so wrapped up in her beauty that they didn't care about anything else but bragging rights to say they were the ones to tap that ass. She could trick them off with the snap of her fingers and they would melt like putty in the palm of her hands giving her anything she wanted.

"Hey." Diamond flirted walking right in between the men focusing her eyes on her target. "What's your name?"

"Pshh." He replied curling his lips as if she carried a pungent odor.

"Maybe you didn't hear me the first time. What's your name sugar?" Diamond said sizing him up.

The man wore an expensive looking watch that shined so brightly it damn near killed her eyes just to look at it. She looked down moving from his feet to his chest realizing that everything he wore had a brand name to it. Lexi stood there giggling at her sister's inability to make this nigga crave her like all the others. She found it amusing that Diamond thought she was God's gift to men and could manipulate them to do her what she wanted them. It was only a matter of time before her little powers wore thin.

"My name huh? Shit everybody knows me baby." The man responded looking past Diamond at a female's chunky ass crossing the street.

"It's Sun, Diamond. You know his name." Lexi said busting her game.

Diamond side eyed her in disgust as she laughed her heart away. She turned her attention back towards Sun leaning in hoping to give him a few whiffs of her Bath and Body Works Cherry Blossom scent.

"Oh so you're Diamond. Yeah, I've heard about you shawty." Sun said licking his lips and checking out her backside.

"You heard about me? Good things, I hope." Diamond responded.

"Yeah you was good alright." Sun laughed along with his associates.

Diamond looked over at Lexi who shrugged back at her. She was beyond embarrassed that they were laughing in her face. She stormed away grabbing Lexi's arm in the process with madness in her eyes.

"Don't go nowhere, baby. I could always use some good head!" Sun yelled to her.

"That's him. That's our victim. We get his bitch ass tomorrow night. He'll be at The Center, I know it." Diamond continued to stomp the pavement.

"What's wrong with you Di? You should be used to niggas calling you a hoe. It's what you do. It's how you make money. Why you trippin' now?" Lexi said snatching her arm away from Diamond's grasp.

Diamond angrily stopped Lexi in her tracks locking eyes with her. "I'm not a hoe. You got that! I'm an opportunist. There's a difference and you're supposed to be my sister, you should know better."

"Know better? Di, we fuck niggas so they give us what we want. What is the term for that? What you need to do is get a grip on reality and see this for what it is." Lexi replied popping her gum and walking off ending the discussion.

Diamond was stuck unable to move after that. Deep down inside of her she knew it was the truth but a piece of her was unable to admit it. She just hated the fact that Lexi put it to her so bluntly. Lexi never turned back after her statement allowing her some time for her thoughts to fester.

She wasn't in the business of kissing her ass when she needed tough love and Diamond needed to be knocked off of her high horse quickly before she floated up into the air like the car in the movie Grease. Lexi wasn't the type of person to sugarcoat anything for anybody, that's just who she was.

****

Pandora sat on the porch thinking about her life and what she would do if she had the type of money Diamond was talking about they could have. She dreamed of going to school to be a psychologist. Helping people sort out their mental problems and social problems was all she loved to do. It was also her way out of having to go see one herself. She figured if she could figure out herself how to help her and her sisters get over the pain and anguish they endured over the years, they would have a fighting chance of becoming upstanding citizens.

Across the street, were the sounds of arguing coming from the porch directly adjacent from Pandora's. She watched as the long time couple had their weekly disagreement over the man's lying cheating ways. He often smacked her around to keep her in line and subservient to his word so she would stay with him. It was pitiful to Pandora. She hated the way he treated her feeling like she was good woman since she never saw her do anything but sit on the porch with her small Chihuahua Fluffy.

"If you did what I said I wouldn't hit you! Now shut the fuck up, I said I'll be back." The man yelled do loud the whole neighborhood could hear him.

"You will not leave and spend three days with that…that whore! I am sick of this Roberto!" The woman shouted with a face full of tears.

Roberto reached down picking up the rake from off the side of his house then leaned it against his shoulder. The woman cowered crouching down on the stoop preparing herself for her usual beating. Pandora raised her head up to get a better look at the situation. Her eyes lowered suddenly feeling a pinch of rage shoot through her. She stood then ran over to the man.

"What the fuck do you think you're doing? You can't hit her like that." Pandora had had enough.

She wasn't about to sit idly by while this man continued to beat this poor innocent woman over and over again and in broad fucking daylight. The woman went over to Pandora standing toe to toe with her and the look on her face was anything but pleased.

"I don't need your fucking help mamacita. This is my husband and I will deal with this on my own." The woman said shooing Pandora away.

"What? Bitch I'm trying to keep him from beating your ass." Pandora retorted.

"I don't need your help. This is our business. Go the fuck across the street!" The woman snapped.

"Well, you need to get your ass whooped in the privacy of your own house and not all out here where people can get involved." Pandora replied.

"P, what's going on?" Diamond asked as she and Lexi walked up to the commotion.

"Girl, nothing just trying to save somebody who don't wanna be saved." Pandora said walking back across the street.

"You always playing captain sav-a-hoe. I done told you about that." Diamond said following behind her.

"I'm just tired of niggas treating women like doormats. Anyway did y'all figure out who y'all gone snatch?" Pandora asked.

"Yeah we got him, P and it's going down tomorrow night." Lexi said two stepping in front of their house.

"Ay, but we need you to get him P." Diamond said walking up the stairs.

"Me? Why me?" Pandora questioned.

"Because you're sweet and innocent. Niggas love bitches like that." Diamond said as she rolled her eyes and darted in the house.

Chapter 3- Execute

Two days had passed since their last run-in with the pastor. He came in and out of the house without so much as a peep. The girls completely stopped all of their chores not even cooking a morsel for him to eat and he still kept quiet. It was shocking to them but they knew it would be short lived just like all the other quiet times.

It was Friday night and Pandora had never really hung out with Lexi and Diamond on their rendezvous' but she was stepping outside of her comfort zone on this night. She knew she had to submit to Diamond and follow her every word in order to be rid of the pastor for good. When they graduated from CVS High School last month, Pandora never imagined that she would be spending her summer partying instead of studying and cleaning.

"Okay Pandora, you're wearing the hell out of it but know that I want my dress back." Diamond said checking her sister out clad in her red Christian Dior dress and black Louboutins.

"Girl this shit ain't even my style. We look like we about to walk the track in this shit you got us wearing." Pandora snapped attempting to pull her skintight dress down.

"Bitch we look sexy! You need to snap out of that old maid phase before you die one." Lexi said shaking her ass to Meek Mill singing Amen.

"Ay, fuck all that. We're here for one purpose and one purpose only. When you seen him, Lex, you let me know." Diamond instructed.

She nodded her head, popping her gum in agreement. Pandora checked her thong for her box cutter making sure her protection was still in place. If any unplanned shit popped off tonight, she would be ready for it. She didn't know these niggas like Diamond and Lexi knew them. In the streets, they were ruthless and heartless assholes who didn't give a fuck about women and treated them like human toilets; shitted on them. Pandora would be damned if she allowed either one of them to disrespect her beauty like that.

The King Center on a Friday night was always popping. It was Juke Night where only the young adults 18-24 could skate and dance until 3am. It was the hottest night of the week for Diamond and Lexi because that's when all the car clubs made their debuts in the parking lot. The Monte Carlo club was full of females and only a hand full of dudes who were all fucking each other within their click.

The Hummer club, were corporate brand niggas who had all of their work logos plastered all over their trucks. They only hollered at chicks that had money already, they were not in the business of taking care of chicks.

Then there was the Lexus club. Whatever these niggas did for a living nobody knew. They could only speculate but they flashed money and spent it like it was going out of style. Kojack and his boys were huddled around their cars blowing back blunts talking loud as hell. He stood about six feet tall and was a light-skinned dude with long dark braids. He stayed fresh to death, never liking an inch of dirt on him or his ride and he never wore the same thing twice. To Diamond his teeth were perfect, his skin was a silky beautiful bronze, and at 24 his body was that of an Adonis. But she was a chicken shit when it came down to ever approaching him. She was afraid her reputation for spreading her legs to the highest bidder might have preceded her.

"Dang, look at Kojack over there Diamond. He's looking too good tonight." Lexi said gyrating her hot little ass around.

"Calm down there, shawty. He's mine." Diamond retorted licking her lips and leaning up against the building.

"Then you'd better snatch him up with yo' scary ass before I show him all this ass I got." Lexi winked at her sister and gave a little smirk.

Diamond never liked to be taunted or forced to do something but her pride wouldn't let her back down. Besides, she knew she had created a monster with Lexi and knew she would go after him if she snoozed.

"I bet you won't fuck him tonight." Lexi laughed as she slowly walked towards him.

"Oh bitch, that's a bet." Diamond snickered, flicking her hair back and rolling her eyes as she strutted over into the hornets nest of dudes.

Lexi stood laughing and shaking her head at how she had punked Diamond into getting over her fear of speaking to him. Even though she wanted him for herself she thought they made a nice odd couple. She turned back to Pandora who was already being hollered at by one of the hard to get Hummer ballers. Lexi smiled at her big sister hoping she finally found her some nicely paid ass. She sauntered over to the gate of the entrance to cop a Yomper from her girls then popped it in her mouth quickly. It was just the fix she needed to keep her sane while she waited on their target to arrive.

"What's good shawty? You looking real good tonight. What you doing over here playing wall flower for?" Tino said enthralled by Pandora's thick waist and smooth legs.

"Thanks." Pandora responded brushing him off.

"What's the matter doll face? Ain't got no man to lick that pussy like you need?"

"What? Nigga don't disrespect me like that! You don't even know me." Pandora snapped.

"Aight shawty. But I got you talking though." Tino said sounding cocky as ever.

Pandora's attitude was off the meter unimpressed by his weak rap and snazzy attitude. She started to walk off but was halted by Tino's hand.

"Okay, okay. You playing hard to get I see. So what's it gonna take to get to know you better?" Tino chuckled reaching into his pocket pulling out a wad of hundred dollar bills.

He licked his index finger then counted the money pretending to ignore her staring off into the distance. Pandora watched his sorry excuse for game then rolled her eyes, sucked her lips revealing a stinky face and stumped past him.

"A better first impression." She snarled walking over to Lexi and her girls.

****

"I'm saying, I know you've been seeing me around. So why you ain't never holler at me?" Diamond spat as she twirled a small portion of her hair around her finger.

"I never noticed you before now, Diamond. Honestly." Kojack shrugged his shoulders.

Diamond's beauty didn't captivate him the least bit. He thought she was very attractive with her dark shaded eyes and blemish free skin. But he was a beast who liked to hunt for his beauty. When women came on too strong he was immediately turned off by that.

She had to admit that his words pierced her soul like a sharp dagger but she wasn't about to show it. Still, Diamond's charm and wit slowly worked it's way into his soul.

"That's okay. You see me now, right?" Diamond asked.

"I see you." Kojack said giving her a slight pinch on her cheek.

Diamond giggled like a little schoolgirl from his touch.

"Com' here Kojack." Diamond flirted.

He leaned down to her allowing her to grab his ears, one of his many sweet spots. She licked his ear seductively then whispered. "I want you."

Kojack leaned back laughing at her remark. She smiled and winked at him but the pounding sounds of bass inside the older model pearl white flip flop Chevy Impala pulling up into the parking lot interrupted her happiness. The 28" chrome Spreewheels slapped the crowd in the face as it entered and pulled up right next to Kojack. Diamond's eyes lit up like a kid in a candy shop. She turned to lock eyes with her sisters posted at the gate, giving them a subtle nod.

"What up fool?" Sun yelled as he exited the car walking straight up to Kojack.

Kojack shook up with him, as did all the other dudes in the lot including Tino, Sun's brother. Diamond wasn't the least bit shocked that Sun and Kojack knew each other, she was however surprised that they were cool since hearing of their prior beef over a money dispute. Supposedly, Sun cheated Kojack out of some big money for some work he had purchased and Kojack wasn't backing down until he got it. Blows were thrown and alliances were broken, but for how long, she hadn't heard but then again it was all hearsay. Her plan wasn't going to work with Kojack in the mix and she damn sure didn't want him knowing about it.

"Hey baby, give me your number and I'll call you later. Alright?" Diamond said trying not to seem anxious as she handed him her IPhone.

Kojack looked down at her hand and laughed again. Her style was amateur at best and it just didn't arouse him not one bit. He found himself mostly attracted to her confidence and drive to get what she wanted. She had that "go-getter" attitude and to him that was the most beautiful trait about a woman. The white Lexis door eased open as Kojack reached in the overhead sun visor snatching one of his business cards from it.

"Jack's Construction?" Diamond said frowning her lips up at him.

"Is that a problem?" Kojack said keeping a watchful eye on Sun as a swarm of chicks surrounded him, each veering for his attention.

"No...uh...not a problem at all." She retorted as she speedily walked back towards her sisters. "I'll call you."

"Tonight." Kojack demanded.

Diamond threw him another wink then shot him a sly smirk as she twisted her hips over to her sisters. The females were swarming around Sun like a hive of honey bees. It was only a matter of time before he chose the ones he wanted to smash for the night.

"Pandora, go get him." Diamond ordered.

"Me? Why me? I don't even know him like y'all do. He's gon' look at me like I'm a lame." Pandora retorted.

"Girl, you are a lame but you're an unknown lame. Lexi is too wired and I can't let my future baby daddy see me hollering at somebody else." Diamond said never taking her eyes off Kojack.

"Duh, we're twins." Pandora snapped.

Inside Pandora was infuriated but she knew it had to be done. She had already agreed to go through with this so there was no turning back now. Her palms became increasingly sweaty by the minute and heart rate began to rise. It was now or never.

"Look P., just do everything how we discussed. You got this." Diamond said encouragingly.

Lexi winked her eye at Pandora nodding her head up and down. Pandora walked slowly towards the crowd where Sun was seemingly being adored. Her heels clicked hard on the concrete but she swore the sound was her heart pounding vigorously. She looked over burning a hole in Sun's face trying to get him to look back at her. He didn't bat an eye at her preoccupied with the amount of pussy dangling around in front of him already. Pandora figured if she kept twisting her ass and giving him the eye that he would soon look up.

Bump!

"Diamond, girl, you betta watch where you going? You actin' like you ain't never seen Sun before." Kojack said grabbing her shoulders to snap her back into focus.

"I'm...I'm..." Pandora hesitated.

She wanted to tell him so badly who she was but his deep Barry White voice melted her soul and moistened her panties a little. His mocha colored eyes danced with hers as he released her and nudged her chin.

"You betta call me, here?" He said smiling at her.

"Mmhmm." Pandora responded now knowing exactly why Diamond lusted after his dreamy ass.

"Hmm. There's something different about you. Did you change clothes?" Kojack asked with a bewildered look on his face.

"Mmhmm."

"I like it. It makes you look thicker in the waist. Nice." Kojack pimped back towards his car with his guys and loaded up.

Pandora watched as they all drove off blasting their sounds rattling every nearby window. Snapping out of her daze she turned to find Diamond scowling at her. She and Lexi were headed straight for her as she huffed and smacked her lips already knowing what was coming.

"Listen Di, I didn't try to. It was an accident and no I'm not tryin' to get with him. He ain't my type." Pandora spat with a funky attitude, waving her hand.

"Really? Hmph. It's cool, girl I wasn't trippin' about that anyway." Diamond retorted with the same attitude as her sister. "Let's go."

Diamond pointed towards Sun giving Pandora a playful push. She smiled at her devilishly and shooed her on. After her steamy run-in with Kojack, she felt like approaching an ugly ass dude like Sun was no problem despite how much money he had. She sashayed over to him like she was the baddest bitch in the crowd pushing all the little skanks out of the way to get to him. He had no choice but to focus in on the creamy caramel beauty walking up to him with thick juicy legs.

"You belong to me." She whispered into his ear then walked towards his Chevy where Lexi and Diamond were already posted.

Sun's dick jumped repeatedly; excited by the seductive way she had caught his attention. It was definitely different from the hanging off the shoulder tugging at his pants bitches he was used to. He needed to know more about this chick as a huge sigh was heard from the groupies he had pryed himself away from and left behind. Sun had a weakness for females but Pandora was no ordinary one. She had spoken to both of his heads not just one like all the other females just trying to get a quick buck.

"Hey. Where you going?" Sun asked running up to her.

Pandora knew she had to keep her confidence in order to keep this ape looking dude drawn to her. She tickled the fully filled beard underneath his chin and continued to silently walk to his car. He was like a puppy dog in her hands though there was something about her that seemed familiar. Whatever it was he was too intoxicated to put his finger on it. As they moved closer to his car, Diamond and Lexi remained out of sight waiting until the right time to reveal themselves.

"Sup, daddy." Lexi said bent over on his hood spreading her ass apart showing him all of her sweet assets.

"Who are you?" Sun was perplexed.

"I'm everything you want and desire baby." She responded walking over to straddle his leg.

"Me too baby." Diamond said emerging from the back of his car.

Their faces looked familiar but all the blunts he had smoked that night fucked his head up and he wasn't thinking straight. All he knew was that they were fine as wine and he needed a taste. His dick jumped again as he used his right hands to calm it down not wanting to startle the ladies before he could get them to his house. He focused his eyes well enough, though, to know that he was indeed seeing double.

"Damn! Twins! Awe shit, get in! Get in the fucking car now!" He said anxiously hitting the unlock button on his key ring.

Chapter 4- R.E.S.P.E.C.T.

Sun gave his brother a fist in the air and honked his horn twice but his face was so wrapped up in tittie central that he didn't even notice his brother's departure. The girls didn't move or speak a lick since Sun had his music blasting Lil' Wayne's Lollipop as they drove on the expressway. What seemed like hours only took about thirty minutes, as they pulled up into the driveway of a huge two-story brick deluxe house, located in the south suburbs of Crete. It was beautiful and clean in this area sort of resembling Beverly only the houses were spaced further apart.

"Let's go ladies." He said popping the locks on the doors for them to exit the car.

They all had their game faces on though each one was playing a different one. It was so dark inside the house that they were almost skeptical about going through with the plan. They didn't know this nigga from Adam or Eve but all the money in the world wouldn't intice them to endanger their lives. Pandora quickly began to have second thoughts as she reached her hands out to feel if her sisters were still around her, they were.

"Follow my voice ladies." Sun yelled from the top of the stairs where a flickering light shone brightly.

"This is some freaky shit." Lexi said as they ventured up the stairs one behind the other.

The room was right across from the stairs with the door cracked midway open. Diamond was done playing games. She smacked her two sisters on the ass and pointed at the door with a vile look on her face. Pandora and Lexi pushed the door open entering to find Sun ass naked lying on the bed with whips and chains adorning the floor. The bed was huge and round with long silver poles attached to it, sitting in the middle of the room and mirrors graced every inch of the walls even the ceiling. Candles were lit to create a seductive ambiance and there were fake rose petals thrown all across the floor.

"Don't be shy, come on in. I haven't used this room in a long time so I lit it up just for you. You should be honored." Sun said slapping his humongous hand down on the bed.

"Shit, you must've thought this was sweet or something. We ain't taking shit off until we see some motherfucking money nigga." Lexi spat still gone off the Yomper.

"The money is right here ladies." He said stroking his long nine-inch super thick dick up and down.

The fact that he had a big dick was nice but none of them could get past his face. If it weren't for him having money he might not have ever gotten any play from females. Diamond stood there with her arms folded and her lips turned up giving the vibe that they were about business. Sun wasn't used to women being so forceful. They usually almost always submitted to him immediately and asked questions later but if he wanted this to happen he knew he was going to have to flash some cash.

"Okay. I'll show you some money since that's the only thing that'll make that pussy drip. But first I wanna see you suck her tits." Sun spat pointing to Lexi and Diamond.

Diamond looked in total disgust. Doing bitches was not her forte and certainly not doing her own flesh and blood. Lexi was silent and still. She figured the show was over right then and there and it was time to go home. Sun got out of the bed and reached under it pulling out a silver suitcase. He opened it revealing a load of cash. He fondled it, throwing it around the room then reached under and pulled out another doing the same thing.

"What the fuck y'all want? Money, cars, clothes? I got all that, baby, that shit is nothing. I know y'all sisters but I wouldn't be tricking if I didn't have it. If you wanna get paid then let's go." Sun said looking down at his feet as a .45 dropped out of the suitcase and onto the floor.

He picked it up as the girls jumped back putting their hands in the air. He waved it off unconcerned with it's presence.

"Y'all ain't gotta worry about that. Shit, I'm just trying to fuck." Sun said walking over to Pandora running his fingers across her nipples making them erect. "Now you suck your sister's tits."

Pandora's pussy tingled with every single touch as he nibbled feverishly on her ear. Diamond nudged Lexi as they laughed at Pandora who was all into the ugly man's advances. They quickly turned their attention on the money scattered everywhere. Their hands immediately began itching with greed and wanting to dive right into it.

"Now do it." Sun demanded interrupting their thoughts.

Lexi faced Diamond standing nose length away from her. She hesitantly reached her hands up grabbing hold of her sister's tits. It was like she was tuning a radio as she winded them back and forth. Diamond couldn't see herself getting into the act at all. She watched as Lexi lowered her dress straps then forcefully yanked them down under her well-developed tits. They sat up and bounced out like perfect little melons as she caressed them as if they were her own and began sucking away at her dark gumdrop nipples.

"Oh my God!" Diamond moaned feeling her sister's tongue flicker back and forth.

It was unimaginable that she could ever feel aroused by something so vulgar. Lexi moved back and forth simultaneously between her tits loving every taste of her blood relative. She moved her hands down under her dress to feel if she was moist, indeed she was. Pandora wanted to vomit right there at the scene. It was like watching a dog take an ugly shit in her mind. It was all she could stand as Lexi and Diamond enjoyed themselves in front of her.

"Now you come over to this bed and get on your knees while I watch that action." Sun demanded, tugging gently at Pandora's hair leading her over to the bed.

The disgruntled look on her face said it all. His dick was curved slightly to the left and it looked like it was having a herpes outbreak on it. She kneeled gawking only at her sisters and keeping a safe distance between her and the seemingly diseased dick.

"Grab it. It don't bite baby." Sun said, smiling.

"The fuck it don't." Pandora retorted.

She said that in her mind but for some reason her mouth felt the need to express it.

"What bitch? You acting funny?" Sun sat up and yelled.

Lexi and Diamond stopped their sexual escapade focusing in on the commotion. They knew it was about to go down and knew their plan had been foiled. The operation was supposed to be clean and swift but it was turning out to be everything but. Diamond saw the blood boiling inside of Pandora, shaking her head at her trying to get her to calm down but it was too late. Being called a female dog sent lightning bolts through her spine.

"Bitch? I got your bitch you blistering dick ass nigga!" Pandora spat attempting to rollback to get up.

Fack!

Sun laid one dead in her jaw sending her to taste the Persian carpet that lay across the floor. He wasn't one to be disrespected by anyone for any reason. He stood there like he was on his pedestal feeling like King Tut of his castle. No bitch would treat him in his own domain. Diamond was fed up with this nigga's antics though and ran up slapping him hard in the face. Nobody fucks with her blood. He was stunned for a brief second but his 220-pound body wasn't phased one bit. He reached his large hand up ready to deliver a powerful pounding to her face.

"Don't move you silly motherfucka!" Pandora said pointing the .45 up to Sun's head.

"Bitch is you crazy? Do you know who I am? Look at my tattoo bitch! I shine brightly around this motherfucka! You done fucked up now dead bitch! All of y'all are dead!" Sun said breathing heavily pointing to his tattoo of an evil looking sun and the words "Shine Nigga" right under it.

"Diamond, Lexi, get this money and put it back in the suitcases. If this sucka even blinks twice his ass is out." Pandora said aiming right between his eyes.

Diamond and Lexi did as they were instructed with no questions. Lexi threw some cash in the one of the cases and as she did spotted three huge white bricks wrapped neatly and packaged side by side. She leaned in to get a better look at what was in the packages but she couldn't tell. Even though she wasn't stupid by far, she couldn't identify what type of drug it was.

"Ay, yo what's this white shit in here?" Lexi asked picking up one of the heavy bricks.

"Well it ain't sugar if that's what you asking." Diamond retorted snatching it out of her hands and throwing it back in the suitcase.

Sun kept his mouth closed. He knew they weren't getting away that easily with his hard earned money. In his mind, it would take more than three bitches to bring his ass down. Diamond and Lexi loaded up the last bit of money then locked the cases and sat them over by the bedroom door. They turned back to see Pandora still standing there staring at Sun. It kind of crept them both out but they were so focused on the fact that they had the money that they weren't thinking about shit else.

"Mount up. We outta here." Pandora said as the ladies walked toward the door.

"But what about him?" Diamond asked looking back at his naked body.

"Leave him." Pandora replied.

"Yeah leave me bitch! I promise you my goons will be on your door step in five minutes shooting up ya crib. Say night night to ya moms and dads bitches!" Sun spat waving his hands angrily.

"He's gonna come after us." Lexi said anxiously.

"No he won't. He's just a bitch ass nigga." Pandora said.

"You right. I'm just as bitch ass nigga and soon I'mma be busting my dick in that sweet little ass watching it bleed as you scream who's the master!" Sun laughed.

"Tsk, Tsk. Watch your mouth when you're in the presence of grown women. Now tie him up with that whip." Pandora ordered.

Diamond grabbed the whip and Lexi wrapped his hands around each other struggling as he tugged away trying to fight it. Pandora pointed the gun right at his temple just in case he thought he would make any sudden moves. Diamond secured the knot around his wrists then tied them to one of his bed poles. They took the blanket from the bed and began wiping everything they touched hoping to have gotten rid of all of their fingerprints.

"Nice ass, though." Lexi said giggling giving his ass a little smack as they headed for the door.

"Dumb ass bitches!" He snapped.

Diamond ran down the stairs first with one case in tow leaving Lexi and Pandora behind. Lexi tapped Pandora on the arm signaling her to follow Diamond but she just stood staring blankly and smiling back at her. She gave her a short nod to go on ahead as Lexi headed down the stairs with the second case. She stood at the front door waiting for Pandora to come down, not wanting to leave her. Pandora's thoughts boiled over ten times. She was tired of raggedy ass niggas like him objectifying women and treating them like whores. He was the whore and he needed to know that.

"You know, if you respected women more, your ugly ass could've had you some pussy." Pandora spat.

"Pussy comes a dime a dozen for me baby. Do you think I'm hurting for that?" Sun retorted.

"But you've never had this kind before baby. See this is the kind that'll make your head spin. This is the kind that makes future senators and presidents. This is not that and that can never be this. It's that virgin pussy baby, and there's nothing else like it around."

"Man, fuck you, BITCH!"

"I just have one question." Pandora laughed. "Do you know Jesus?"

Pandora stuffed the .45 in her left bra strap then walked over jumping on top of the bed behind him using his underwear from the floor to cover his mouth. She pulled his neck back slipping the box cutter out of her thong with ease. His screams were muffled yet the piss coming from his dick made it apparent that he was terrified of what was about to happen to him. Sun squirmed and fought as much as he could trying to get her off of him. A creepy smile filled her face as she gripped his mouth tightly then slit his neck from ear to ear with one steady slash, sending a gush of blood flying around the room. His body dropped like a bag of ice as gargling sounds sluggishly dissipated from the wound and Pandora ran out like a thief in the night.

****

It was dead time and they were walking down an eerie road in a part of town they weren't familiar with. The night's wind was brisk but still tolerable growing goose bumps on their skin and to top it all off Pandora had a hand drenched in blood. She took the box cutter and stomped it into the ground of an abandoned field then wiped her hand on the leaves of a nearby tree. Her sisters watched out while she cleaned herself ripping the leaves up and letting them blow in the wind. The little bit of blood that was left was just enough for her to hide until she got home to bathe.

"HEY!" Lexi yelled flagging down a cab, waving her hands. "Ugh! That son of a bitch could've stopped."

They kept walking headed for the gas station they were staring down the road. It was so dark that they could barely see the long blades of grass surrounding them and the road wreaked of old motor oil and country meadows. The night air grew colder as air sifted up their skimpy dresses. It seemed like they had been walking forever without any cars in sight. Diamond's heel began to crack as bright lights shone from behind them becoming closer and closer with every step. They turned around to see it was the same cab they had tried to flag down a few minutes ago.

"Hey, hey. Where you pretty ladies going?" The older man said looking at them from out the top of his thick paned glasses.

"Can you take us to Evergreen Plaza?" Diamond spoke up.

"Damn! That's pretty damn far lil' lady. I'm not sure you got the cash for that. I don't got no credit card machine." He replied.

"Don't worry. We got this." Pandora retorted confidently.

Chapter 5- Butterflies

The next morning after the murder the TV stations were lit on fire with the news about the death of local dope dealer Sun Andrews. Lexi was the first to catch the spot and couldn't believe her ears when she heard it. She didn't think it would be the talk of the town so quickly. Her heart beat a mile a minute, almost flying up out of her chest. The bottom of her feet felt like they were cemented to the floor and her mouth was open wide enough for a hawk to fly in it.

"Pandora and Diamond! Y'all better come see this shit, yo." Lexi yelled.

"What chick? I was about to take a hot shower." Pandora said annoyed at how urgent she sounded.

"You sure gonna need one after this. Check it out." Lexi said pointing to the TV screen. "Where's Diamond?"

"I have no idea."

Pandora stood as they described the gory scene that they left at Sun's house that night. She stared at the screen feeling a sense of victory that she was the one to get that scumbag off the street. It seemed the police wasn't going to do anything about it so she did. She didn't have a problem with the fact that he sold drugs just that he didn't respect women at all. She had dealt with abusive, domineering men all of her life so getting rid of Sun was nothing to her.

"Turn that crap off. You don't need to be filling your head with bullshit like that." She said waving it off and plopping down on Lexi's bed.

"It's not crap girl. It's informative. We need to keep watch on the progression of the case, don't ya think?"

"No. I don't think. You need to get your head out of this shit because the more you think about it the more you think about ratting and I know you don't want to do that. Right lil' sis?" Pandora said pointing her finger all in Lexi's face.

Lexi jumped a bit wondering what was her angle. Pandora had a look in her eye that she had never seen before. It was a look of desperation, of pure sinister evil. She wasn't fond of it at all and pushed her hand away from her. It was pissing her off and she wasn't in the mood to get into it with her right then. Pandora backed off but still gave Lexi the eye to let her know she wasn't playing with her. She wasn't about to down for murder because some little girl had butterflies in her stomach. They all just needed to keep it cool with the their regular routines and lay low for a while until things killed over.

"Besides, if I go down we all go down. You were all there so you are all in it. Got me?" Pandora continued.

"Yeah sis. I got you."Lexi replied. "Weren't you going to take a shower or something?"

Pandora gave her the side eye wondering why she wanted to get rid of her so badly now. She left the room in search for her cell phone so she could call Diamond and find out where she was. The room was silent except for her feet scraping the floor from all of the pacing back and forth that would have drove a monkey crazy. Her fingers frantically dialed the number anxiously waiting for her to answer.

"Yeah." Diamond answered.

"Where the fuck are you?" Pandora asked slowing her breathing.

"I'm with a friend. What the hell is wrong with you?"

"Mmhmm. Have you seen the news Diamond?"

"Naw girl. I've been sleep most of the day. What's on it?" Diamond asked worriedly.

"Just that shit that happened." Pandora said sitting down on her bed.

"Oh right. Well what do you want to do?" Diamond asked hoping for the answer she so desperately wanted to hear.

She wanted to move to California and live the rich and glamorous life. Chicago was cool and it would always have a place in her heart but she felt like she would be a fool if she didn't go out there to see what else the world had to offer. But her sisters were so stuck on remaining in Chicago that everyday it seemed like they were never going to get out of that city.

"Nothing. I think Lexi is losing it." Pandora said.

"Awe, no. I think she's good. You know you don't have to worry about her. Shit she pops too many Yompers to crack under pressure. It sounds like you're losing it though. Are you okay?" Diamond asked with a bit of concern in her voice.

"What? Yeah girl I'm too cool. There's nothing wrong over here. I'm straight." Pandora replied.

The fact that she kept repeating virtually the same thing over and over again with laughter made Diamond think she was going to crack under pressure. She sat on the phone for a few minutes giving Pandora time to collect her thoughts before she replied to her obvious lie.

The nigga in the seat next to her was just about to pull in the IHOP parking lot and signaled for her to wrap up her conversation so they could eat.

"So you're good then, P?" Diamond asked again to make sure.

"Girl, what? If you think I'm bugging you got another thing coming. I just wanted to know if you thought something was up with Lex. I swear I would hate for anything to have to happen to her." Pandora said sounding shifty.

"Huh? What could happen to her?"

"Naw, naw. I was just saying if she mysteriously disappeared." Pandora said with her voice becoming lower and lower and the inflection her voice changing.

"Okay Pandora. See now you scaring me. Are you thinking of getting rid of Lex? Is that what you're asking me?

"No. Why would I ask you that? I was just saying some things that got me off my square. Ya know?" Pandora replied.

"Don't do anything rash, P. We're your sisters and we will love you no matter what. Don't ever think that we aren't here for you.

"Are you Diamond?"

"Am I what P?"

"Here for me?"

"What do you think, Pandora? I wouldn't do half of the shit that I do for you."

"Yeah well…whatever."

"Well alright P. I'll see ya when I get there."

Diamond hung up the phone before she could even respond. She had a good night all night and was about to have an even better afternoon so she wasn't prepared to ruin her day with her nonsense. Pandora put the phone down on the bed, realizing that she was indeed the one tripping off of the afternoon news. She had the home court advantage over both of her sisters because they were afraid of what she might do to them if they crossed her.

****

"You know if my wife ever found out about us she would kill you." Brian said leaning in to kiss Diamond on her cheek.

"Whatever nigga. I ain't trying to hear that shit. First off she'll have to catch me and she'll get to you before she gets to me." Diamond laughed stuffing eggs in her mouth.

"True, true." He said shrugging his shoulders. "But she'll never find out now will she?"

Brian pinched her cheek like she was a cute chubby little baby. Diamond hated that but he was so sexy that she overlooked everything he did. Not only was he sexy but also he dropped that cash to her like she was a human bank. Whenever she needed anything he got it for her. But now that they were set she didn't need his money, she just wanted it and his dick. Brian was a shorty standing only at 5'5" but his physique was that of the world's strongest bodybuilder.

He had the sexiest mocha colored eyes and the firmest ass of any of her men. He was middle aged and kept only a mustached face and a clean bare chest even though he was extremely hairy. It was the way Diamond liked it so it kept like that for her.

"She will only find out if you can't keep your mouth closed. Anyway, why are talking about her? I'm trying to enjoy my breakfast not barf all over it." Diamond cackled.

"Barf? My wife is as beautiful as you are baby. So don't get it twisted. Shit I'm trying to get y'all in the bed together. That's like the ultimate fantasy." He replied chomping down on two slices of bacon at the same time.

"I've said it once and I'm saying it again. I don't fuck with bitches. Stop asking me. I told you I don't get down like that." Diamond snapped putting her fork down. "And if your wife is so fucking perfect than why are you here with me and not at home waking up to her?"

Brian hated when she talked like that. He knew he shouldn't have been there with her but it was something about her he couldn't get past. Since the first day she met him, doing off duty security work at the gas station on 79th and Pulaski, he couldn't get her out of his mind. He had to have her and pursued her at every chance he got. In the beginning, she was far from interested but when he offered to buy her any and everything she wanted just to spend a little time with her, that's when he fucked up. From then on he had her attention even if he did have to pay just to get it.

"Because I chose not to. That's why. She thinks I'm in East Chicago, Indiana anyway with my brother at his bachelor party." He replied.

"Well, she can have you back when I'm done with you anyway. I just need to go get my hair and nails done and then I need a new Gucci purse. Do you think you can handle that today?" She asked.

"Damn girl. Shit these weekly rendevous' to the Hilton is killing me enough already because you just won't do it in anything less than stellar and now you want Gucci and shit?" Brian said raising his eyebrows at her as if she had lost her mind.

"Excuse me?"

He could see it all in her face that he had fucked up just that quickly. Diamond sat quietly finishing her food gazing at everything around her that wasn't him. Brian didn't watch anything but her though wondering if her silence would dissipate soon. He hadn't tried to make her mad but he was working triple double over time just to support his wife's lifestyle and hers. But the treatment was killing him and he wasn't ready to give up his young piece of tail just yet.

"Alright, Diamond. We can go to Gucci." Brian said in a dry voice.

"And to get my hair and nails did?" She asked.

"Of course, my darling. Anything for you."

Diamond's eyes lit up, making her happier than ever. She didn't feel sorry for him since it was his choice to keep fucking her when he had pussy at home already. He was going to have to pay like he weighed and if that was too little than he'd have to put on a few pounds. She was heartless about hers especially since she had put in work overtime for him last night and got little to no sleep.

"You damn right anything for me. Now let's go." Diamond said getting up from the table.

She walked outside of the restaurant waiting for him to finish clearing the bill when her cell rang again. The number was all too familiar but she didn't really want to talk to him right now. He was a forty five year old married man who was becoming clingy like a high school virgin who had just had his virginity broken. At first fucking him was a ton of fun because he liked to dress up in leather and chains and let her beat him like he stole something. She was his exotic beautiful dominatrix and she fulfilled every fantasy he had. But she grew tired of screwing his old ass after merely three months but she strung him along as a backup plan. He dropped that cash hard on her too. Most times she didn't even have to ask for it, he would just lower $500 at a time and tell her to go by something pretty. She liked the fact that she didn't have to ask for it.

"Yeah, Bill." She reluctantly answered.

"Hey darling. I hadn't heard from you in about a week now. I need to know what's going on." He recited his thick country accent.

"Well…Bill…I've been mighty busy sugar. I've been squaring all my ducks in a row so I can move into my own place you know."

"Diamond, I don't give a shit if you were combing your hair straight. I need to see ya gal."

"What did you just call me? You know I hate that damn word. Do you want me to hang up on you, huh, Bill? Is that what you want?" Diamond spat in her dominatrix voice.

"No. No not at all madam. I'm sorry. I truly am. I just wanna know if I can sees ya. That's all." Bill replied shuttering the thought of her rejection.

"Then I suggest you wait on my call." Diamond said startled by Brian's presence.

"Who you talking to?" Brian asked grabbing her shoulder.

"Uh, nobody baby. Just pull the car around now." Diamond responded with a smile placing the phone to her knee.

"Sure don't sound like nobody." Brian said, shaking his head and walking ff to find his car in the crowded parking lot.

"Hello? Diamond? Hello?"

"Yes Bill. I'm here. Now you must do as I say. Go fuck your wife and I'll call you tomorrow."

"What? I don't want that old shriveled up thang I want you dammit." Bill said becoming angry.

"Do it or when I see you I'm going to give you the pounding of your life. Do you hear me boy?" Diamond replied just the way he liked it.

"Yes madam."

"Ugh." She uttered after hanging up the phone.

Brian pulled his Lincoln MKX right up in front of her then popped the locks for her to jump in. Now it was his turn to play the silent treatment game. Diamond knew he had an attitude but she hadn't catered to him ever before and she sure wasn't about to start now. The look on his face was priceless though, and she had to admit it was very sexy. She didn't know what it was about married men that drove her crazy, they just had an aura that single men didn't display.

"So you not gon' tell me who you was on the phone with?" Brian asked looking out the window.

"Damn. Are you that mad about it?" Diamond laughed hysterically. "Fine, B. It was my daddy. Are you happy now?"

"You're daddy, huh?"

"What you don't believe me? Would you like to call him yourself?" She asked handing him her Iphone.

"Naw. Just try not to talk to your *daddies* in front of me. Ya heard?" Brian laughed knowing she was lying.

That small blow to Diamond's ego pissed her off royally but she was willing to let it go for the sake of her shopping spree for the day.

She slipped her phone back in her skirt pocket then stared out of the window to avoid saying anything she might have regretted in the future. She knew what she was doing and had each of her financial sponsors in check.

His remark, however, poked a hole in the bubble she sat on top of. She figured she was the baddest bitch around, remaining untouchable to many and only available to some. He was no better than her being married and sleeping around. It was only a sign of the times that sooner or later she would have to cut his ass off too.

Chapter 6- You're Mine

Knock. Knock.

"Sup, P. You busy?" Diamond asked slipping in Pandora's room door.

Her room was very empty because the pastor never bought them anything. They each had a plain wooden dresser with a mirror attached and a twin-sized bed with basic ordinary cotton sheets and a thin comforter to keep them warm in the winter months. The only thing major about their rooms was their clothes and that's because Diamond usually had niggas buy gear for them.

"Naw, what's up?" Pandora replied sliding $300 into her brand new leather Coach wallet.

She closed the suitcase then signaled for Diamond to turn her head as she strategically hid it under her bed. She had it booby trapped with wire duct tape so she would know if it had been messed with. It wasn't that she didn't trust her sister's not to steal any of the money; it was just that she needed to be in control of it seeing as though it was such a large quantity. She knew that if they had control over it they would just spend it on worthless material shit instead of trying to better themselves with it.

Diamond had a good plan but Pandora felt like hers won them the jackpot to ensure they would be comfortable outside of the pastor's domain. She wasn't about to let no one ruin that.

"It's been 3 days and I still haven't talked to Kojack. I'm scared because that shit from the other night has been all over the news. Plus, he told me to call him that night but I couldn't." Diamond said biting on her nails and twirling a portion of her hair.

"Don't worry about that, Di. He's not gonna care. He'll just think you were playing hard to get or something. Just call the nigga, dang. You ain't never had a problem before. Don't act brand new now." Pandora said waving her off.

She stood slipping her jeans on and ruffled through her closet for her pink shimmering halter-top and slid it on as well. She took out her pink open toed wedges, sliding her feet in effortlessly.

"Well…um…you not worried about that shit from the other night, P?" Diamond asked trying not to sound like a lame.

Pandora felt that question coming. She had this newfound confidence about herself since that night feeling like she was untouchable, like she was on top of the world running things and handling business. She had opened up a Chase bank account and planned to deposit money every week like it was her job check.

They had begun looking at apartments and preparing to move out and on with their lives. It had only been a few days but already the power in the house had shifted dramatically.

"No. As long as you two remain sleep, everything is good." Pandora said spraying Burberry on her neck.

"Right, right." Diamond replied squashing the conversation.

"Where's Lex?" Pandora stopped to ask.

"Out as usual."

"Hmph. I'm gone to sign the lease on this apartment up north. I'll be back shortly." Pandora said muffing Diamond in the head and walking out the door.

She tussled her hair fixing it back to its normal state then laid in Pandora's bed on her stomach. She pulled her Iphone from out of her skirt pocket along with Kojack's business card staring at it dreamily. The numbers on the phone seemed to become bigger and bigger, though, with each one she dialed. Her heart rate sped up and sweat formed on her forehead as the phone began to ring.

"What's good?" Kojack's voice sounded sweeter than it did the other night.

"Hi darling." Diamond spat slipping charm in her voice.

"Who is this?"

"Diamond. You don't remember?" She said looking confused.

"Oh yeah. What happened to you, man?" He asked.

"I got caught up in some business. But anyway, what's up with you?" Diamond retorted trying to change the subject quickly.

"Man, I'm out here on the block. Motherfuckas trying to figure out who done up Sun like that. I know you heard about it." Kojack said.

"Yeah it's all on the news. Say they split him wide open, huh?" Diamond spat.

"Shit, hell yeah. He was a bitch but he ain't deserve to go out like that, you know. But anyway what's up wit' you shawty? You comin' through or what?"

"When you want me, Kojack?"

"Shit, where you at? I'll come swoop you right now. We can go eat or something." Kojack spat back at her.

"Or something, huh?" Diamond laughed.

She was all for the "or something" and desperately wanted it to happen too. There were footsteps coming up to the door as she turned and stared into the pastor's face. He stood there as if he wanted to say something but never spoke a word. Diamond wasn't in the mood for his bullshit so she ignored him rolling her eyes and turning back over continuing with her conversation.

"Um, why don't I meet you tonight at the Applebee's in Evergreen. We can eat there." She whispered hoping the pastor hadn't heard her plans.

"Damn girl. I could come swoop you and we can spend the rest of the day together now. I'm not like other niggas just hit it and quit it, ya feel me? I at least give you time to show me you're a hoe before I treat you like one." Kojack spat.

"I love the way you talk." Diamond said before realizing she had blurted it out loud. "Shit."

"Ah, don't trip ma. It's all-good. Aight, just meet me tonight at 8."

"I got you."

Diamond hung up the phone cheesing like the Cheshire cat. She was ecstatic to finally have talked to him and to learn that he wasn't even mad about the other night. The pastor was still in the doorway staring at her with his arms folded leaning against the wall. His look was solemn; there was no emotion at all. It was almost like he was dead. Diamond got off the bed and attempted to walk out the door but he stopped her in her tracks pushing her backward.

"Where are your sisters?" He asked quietly.

"I don't know." Diamond spat, smacking her lips and rolling her eyes with an attitude.

"Where are you going?"

"No where. Leave me alone." Diamond yelled as she tried to storm past him.

"Leave you alone! You are my fucking daughter! I don't have to leave you alone and I have a right to know where you're going and with whom." The pastor said walking towards her with his finger pointed in her face.

Diamond tried to dip past him but it was no use. For an old man he was just as quick and agile as she. He grabbed her by the arms but she broke away pushing him into the dresser. He had underestimated her youthful strength.

"Don't fucking touch me again! You're not my daddy. You ain't shit to me!" Diamond yelled.

"How are you going to tell me? Yes you are. You're my daughter. I signed your birth certificate. I was there when you were born." He said.

"Yeah but you weren't there when we were conceived motherfucka. Momma cheated on your dumb ass cause she was sick and tired of your bitch ass so she went out and found a real man," Diamond said, laughing in his face, "and as far as her letters are concerned my daddy's dick was fire!"

The pastor became enraged. He didn't know if she was lying but her words burned through him like an incinerator. There was always that thought in the back of his mind since the girls never really came into his looks but he put it aside because he loved her that much.

"Yeah. Lex is yours but Pandora and I are not from your ratchet seed. So, now you know. Deal with that." Diamond said as she strutted towards the door.

Diamond was confident she had won this round. She had finally gotten the upper hand on the pastor and soon he would be left to wallow in his own misery. She couldn't wait for Pandora to come back with the keys to their new place so they could dangle them in his face and move out that night.

Shock filled her face as the pastor reached up and grabbed her by the neck tightly. He shook her as he choked her lifting her up off the ground leaving her feet to dangle in the air. His face was filled with bloodthirsty anger and confusion. Diamond felt life slipping away from her gradually as she clawed at his fingers trying to pry them from her neck.

She gasped for air but it only made him squeeze even tighter. He finally just threw her on the bed as she coughed heavily struggling to get a hold of herself. The pastor climbed on top of her, slapping her down to the bed hard with his hand. Diamond kicked and punched at him as hard as she could, trying to make sure he didn't get what he had came for. She reached up scratching him in his eyes and cheeks like she was clawing her way out of a buried casket but it didn't seem to stop him. He tugged at her thin t-shirt ripping it straight down the middle. Then he covered her mouth with one hand applying an immense amount of pressure to hold her down and with his other hand unbuckled his slacks releasing his Johnson.

He fixed himself in between her legs putting all his weight on her so she could barely move. Diamond kicked and screamed, though muffled and restrained, for her freedom.

"Stop!" She screamed through his hand. "Don't do this! No!"

Her cries went unanswered and unheard as he stretched her panties to the side rubbing his limp dick on her warm hairless snatch.

"Shut the fuck up! Shut up!" He said waiting for his dick to get hard.

Diamond fought his forcefulness as much as she could but he never budged an inch. He finally became hard enough to penetrate and slowly inserted himself inside of her squeezing the head to make it stiff enough to enter and without even thinking about protection. The pastor moaned deeply once fully inside as he began moving back and forth closing his eyes in enjoyment. Her pussy was so warm and inviting that he almost lost himself in her wetness. Diamond sat there without a sound and without emotion. She refused to give him the benefit of the doubt that he had broken her since he took what he wanted without reservation.

"God is going to forgive me for this if you are my child but if you aren't then take this dick bitch!" He chanted over and over again as if it were one of his psalms.

He shoved and rammed himself inside of her faster and harder every time maneuvering her legs around to the best feeling position. She only wanted to breathe. She felt that as long as she was still alive that's all that matter. Her body was a shell, he could have that, but he would never take her inner being, her soul. He reached down taking out one of her tits from her bra revealing the prettiest dark gumdrop nipples he had ever seen. They were better than Vivian's even. His dick grew harder leaning his head in to lick it with his tongue dancing all around it. His hot breath reeked of beer and corn nuts but it didn't stop him from breathing a mouthful into her face.

Diamond prayed that one of her sisters would come in and stop the madness soon. She didn't know how much longer she would be able to hang on without purposely causing vomit for her to choke on.

****

"Hey Keisha. What's all this about?" Pandora asked walking up to her best friend's house grabbing a seat on the porch.

Keisha lived in the heart of the hood on 55th and Garfield, their old neighborhood before their mother afforded to move them into a better environment. Her and Keisha remained friends, though, never losing touch. She was the only child and a huge square who was overweight from depression and who never liked to go anywhere or do anything. Keisha's mother was sick with cervical cancer so there were more bad days than good. She rarely wanted to enjoy life since her mother wasn't able to do so. The biggest thrill she ever got was sitting on the porch and collecting the scoop on the neighborhood gossip. Most of it was just rumors and by the time it got back to the person involved it was a brand new story. It was like a real life soap opera right outside her door.

"Girl, the folks are trying to figure out who done up Sun the other night. Girl his brother Tino is over there and everything. I don't know but they say that they fucked him in the ass and everything, girl." Keisha rambled on.

Pandora laughed at the way rumors spread and stories got switched around before people heard the truth. She knew her girl was the human informant but this time her story wasn't straight and wanted to tell her so badly what the real deal was. The thing was Keisha couldn't hold water even if you sewed her peel hole up tight and let her rot form thirst.

"Girl, none of that happened." Pandora laughed hysterically.

"Shit, how do you know?"

"Cause girl. Ain't nobody want that shit." Pandora continued to laugh drawing attention to herself.

Tino looked over onto the porch noticing who she was. He had a right mind to go over to her and play it cool so he could smash something beautiful to ease his pain but he knew he couldn't abandon his mission for a soft piece of ass. Even though he and his brother didn't see eye to eye all the time, he was still his only little brother and he loved him dearly. Tino knew he wasn't going to be able to leave; he just couldn't bring himself to do it. He looked over and saw Kojack looking at the same thing he was.

"What you looking at fool?" He said sarcastically.

Kojack grew up with Sun and Tino since they were babies. Their dads used to work together and became best friends prompting their sons to follow suit. But as the years went by they took separate paths and greed took over leaving them split as peas in a pod. Though despite any disagreements they may have had over the years they learned to stick together against all odds.

Kojack, however, was slowly drifting from that pact. He was on to bigger, better, and more positive things while they were moving in the opposite direction. A direction in which Kojack didn't have time for. Now with Sun gone, he knew Tino would try to stick to him like glue.

"Nothing, nigga. Ay, I'll be right back." Kojack said hustling across the street following his eyes.

Pandora watched in awe as Kojack neared her and Keisha on the porch. Her palms were sweaty and her feet grew weak wanting to fall out so he would go away but that would've been too embarrassing. He walked up to the short silver gate in front of the house and leaned on it grinning widely at Pandora and waving hello to Keisha, showing respect.

"So this is why you couldn't meet up, huh?" He said with the side eye.

"Huh...oh yeah. Gotta kick it with my girl." Pandora retorted not having the foggiest idea of what he was talking about.

"Well, Keisha is my girl too so what I'm going to say won't offend her." Kojack stood taking out his Evo punching buttons profusely. "Let's Go. You coming with me."

"Huh? Wait...I can't leave Keish like that. That ain't cool." Pandora said.

"Awe. P—" Keisha fell back on her butt being pushed down rudely by Pandora.

She didn't have time to explain to Keisha the reason why she cut her off but if she had let her finish her sentence her cover would have been blown right then and there. Pandora wasn't ready for him to find out quite yet that she wasn't the person he thought she was. She thought for sure he would be less enamored with the real her and leave her to go find the real Diamond. It wasn't a rejection she was willing to deal with. When she told him it had to be on her time and her way so that she could have a fighting chance of keeping hm. If she could get him to fall in love with her, she knew he would never leave her, ever.

"You know what, on second thought, I will come with you. See ya, Keish." Pandora interrupted smiling and waving back at her.

She ran down the stairs following behind Kojack as he walked to his car. Her feet could not move fast enough as she hurried looking back giving Keisha the signal that she would call her later. Down the street, a few houses away, Lexi sat on another porch kicking it with some of her old friends and popping Yompers. She squinted really hard making sure her eyes weren't deceiving her before she realized she was right. She saw Pandora hop her ass in the car with Kojack.

"Ooooo." Lexi said shaking her head as she watched them ride off into the horizon unnoticed.

Chapter 7- Where were you?

Kojack cruised down Lake Shore Drive, enjoying the cool summer breeze against his face. His laid-back demeanor spoke volume as Pandora relaxed in the seat feeling like she had known him for years. She didn't even bother to ask where they were going. He could have been taking her to a ditch to kill her and she would have been none the wiser. The atmosphere was just that comfortable. They pulled up into the crowded parking lot of 57th Street Beach. After scrambling around like roaches for a few minutes, they settled on a nice parking spot with lots of shade and a perfect view of the lake. It was a great relief from the near 90° degree weather.

"This is nice." Pandora said staring at the beautiful view of Lake Michigan.

"Yeah." Kojack spat staring at Pandora like he wanted to sop her up with a biscuit.

"What is it?" Pandora asked noticing his gaze.

"What's what?" He asked coolly.

"Nothing." Pandora laughed.

Kojack leaned against his car pulling her by the front of her shirt close in between in his legs. He wrapped his strong cut arms around her small frame, caressing her hips running his fingertips along her lower back being sure not to touch her ass. He didn't want to set her off or disrespect her in anyway. She smiled as she dug her head into his chest feeling all warm and fuzzy inside. Pandora had only ever dated two boys in high school and they had never made her feel the way she felt when she was with him. They had never touched or even looked at her the way he did.

"From the second moment I saw you, I knew you were the one for me. This shit just feels right." Kojack whispered smelling the vanilla scent of her soft hair.

"The second moment?" Pandora asked raising one eyes brow.

"Yeah. I mean the first time you were cute and all but you was a little annoying, too. You came on strong as hell ma, real talk. I thought you just wanted to hit it and beat it." Kojack pulled her face from the buried position in his chest. "But the second time, when you bumped into me, it was like magic. I was hooked."

"I don't think I've ever heard a man say anything so beautiful before." Pandora damn near swooned in his arms.

"See that's why I'm feeling you. You're not like other chicks, you know, you're not ghetto. You recognized me as a man and not a nigga. You know a real man when you see one and that's love boo." Kojack spat.

He pulled her in squeezing tightly never wanting to let her go. All of his years of looking for the right woman and now he had felt like his search was finally over. Pandora wasn't even thinking about the deceit that she had used to get him. All she could think about was how good his masculine arms felt wrapped around her torso.

"You ready to get something to eat?" Kojack whispered.

"I'm already full." Pandora replied.

****

The pastor arched his back releasing his seeds all inside of her. Diamond thought she had died and gone to hell the first couple of times he mounted her. But after the third time she was certain she was living right in the middle of it. He rammed himself inside of her deep then fell on top of her like dead weight letting out a faint snore. His head was pressed heavily on her chin as she stared blankly at the wall unable to speak or breathe.

"You sure inherited one thing from your lying ass momma." He awoke suddenly whispering into her ear, sticking his tongue down the inner of it.

Diamond cringed throwing her weight, shifting over hoping he would fall off and release her.

"Do you feel like a man? Huh? Did fucking me make you feel good about yourself?" Diamond spat clearing her throat.

He looked at the side of her face with a twisted look upon his. She knew she was egging on his anger but she didn't give a fuck. In her mind, he was beneath her like scum on the bottom of her shoe. He could kill her dead right then and he would still be the scum of the fucking earth to her. He reached down anxiously stroking his weak schlong preparing it for yet another round. Diamond's words were just the fuel he needed, prompting him to continue his act on her. He wanted to break her even if that meant he had to break himself to do it.

"You know you've got some nice ass titties too. I should bust all over them." The pastor said grabbing a hand full and placing the nipples in his mouth one by one. "Or maybe I should aim for that pretty little mouth."

His tongue went outside of his lips licking in a circular motion like he was hungry for his last meal. He leaned in to kiss her letting his tongue lead the way to her mouth. Diamond rocked her head back and forth refusing to let his vile serpent mingle its saliva with hers. He grabbed her chin roughly pulling it straight, planting his crusty big lips on hers while fingering around with her youthful clitoris. She tried not to let out any sounds as she jerked with every flicker he bestowed upon her. His stale saliva smelled like mildew on her skin on the outside of her mouth. She opened her mouth pretending to accept his tongue inside then extended her head reaching to bite down on his lip. Diamond failed to grab it in time and her attempt ignited the pastor's anger even more.

He bit down hard on hers in retaliation, laughing the entire time.

"Ahhh!" Diamond screamed in agony as he slipped back inside of her.

"Oh! That's how I make you scream, huh? I gotta bite ya." The pastor retorted smiling like he had just won a Nobel Peace Prize. "Well, since you like that let me do it again."

He bit down on her lip again making sure to do it even harder this time, attempting to draw blood. Diamond let out an excruciating scream as tears flowed from her eyes from the pain. He was pleased with himself as he continued to bang out her virtuous pussy. Diamond was beyond pissed that he had finally broken her silence. She didn't feel as though she had the upper hand over the situation anymore. It tore her up inside as he started to laugh sinisterly at her cries.

"I hate you motherfucka! I fucking hate you!" Diamond spat hearing his laughter grow louder and louder.

He leaned his head back with excitement. Though he was tired, her cries were the fuel he needed to keep his act going. His pumping sped up like he was about to bust inside of her harder than he had ever done with anyone before then he abruptly stopped. He fell on top of her hard almost bumping heads. Diamond looked around unable to see anything but the ceiling as his body weight began to crush her small physique. It was as if he had died right on top of her, remaining stiff as a board, seemingly not breathing.

"Di, are you okay?" Lexi said rolling the pastor off of her and dropping the thick metal pole from her hands.

"Oh my fucking God! It's about time y'all showed up. Where's Pandora?" Diamond asked wiping her tears and fixing her clothes then looking down at the sorry ass bastard.

"I don't know. Let's just get the fuck outta here." Lexi spat pulling her arm trying to lead her out the door.

"NO! We can't leave the shit and I don't know where Pandora is hiding it. Let's just tie this fool up and call this bitch. Let her know to get her a-sap." Diamond retorted signaling for her to grab the pastor's arms while she reached for his legs.

****

"I know you said you wanted to go to AppleBee's, but that lobster was killer though, wasn't it?" Kojack said opening the car door for her.

As they left the Tru Restaurant parking garage downtown, Pandora looked at him realizing she had no idea what he was talking about, Applebee's. She figured Diamond must have called him like she said she would to set up a date. She nodded her head in agreement. It was in fact the best lobster she had ever tasted; way better than the mediocre ones at Red Lobster. Kojack was the perfect gentleman the whole night, opening doors and allowing her to sit before him. She wasn't aware that there were men out there who were willing to be every woman's fantasy.

"I had a great time tonight." Pandora said reaching over to touch his hand laying hers across his.

He locked his fingers with hers then brought her hand up towards his mouth, kissing it gently. Pandora wanted to melt right there. This man was higher, deeper, tighter, flyer than anyone she had ever known. His inner being was speaking to her without any words and she knew hers spoke back. It was a lovely dance their bodies were performing without even being on the floor. It was real. So real that no labels or titles could describe what was going on between them.

"What do you mean had? You know it doesn't have to end, right?" Kojack spat.

"I...I have to take care of some business." Pandora replied quietly.

"Business, huh? Is that business more important than what's happening right here, right now?" Kojack asked in a stern tone.

Leaving him was the last thing she wanted to do. A part of her didn't want to answer the question. She had just signed a lease on a brand new condo in the River North area and she wanted to break the news to her sisters that they could move out tonight. She wanted to let them know that the hell they had lived all of their lives was finally over and that she would die before they fell to the pastor's feet again. Kicking it with Kojack was a major plus to her day but she owed it to Lexi and Diamond to get them out of there.

"Baby, I'm feeling this. I really am but I gotta go." Pandora felt herself pleading like he was holding her captive.

"Damn, Diamond. I'm feeling this shit too and I don't want it to end…not right now."

Hearing him call her by that name scorched her soul. It was wrong for her to be there, adoring him, when she knew he was supposed to belong to her sister. But it didn't seem fair to her. Diamond got everything. She got all the niggas attention with her seductive ways and they bought her damn near everything she wanted. It was time for the Earth's crust to shift in her favor and she would start with him. She loved her sister, no doubt, but she was done putting her happiness on hold. Kojack had made it blatantly clear that she was his so he would be hers, at all cost.

"Stay with me tonight." Kojack said.

"Tonight?" Pandora asked.

"No, I'm not gonna think you're a ho. Man, we ain't even gotta do nothing. I just wanna be with you, get to know you, all that."

"Damn, Kojack." Pandora shook her head smitten by how wonderful he was.

"If you can't, I'll understand. But I can't promise I won't be hurt." Kojack poked his lip out making puppy dog eyes and whimpering sounds.

It was the cutest thing she had ever seen. How could I say no? She thought feeling on fire for this man. It was even more than sex it was mental. It was that alone that attracted her to him but now her physical was beginning to feel neglected as well. The tingling she felt run through her body yearned for his touch.

In society's eyes it would be so wrong but tonight she would feel so right.

"There's no where else I'd rather be than here with you." She leaned over into his ear and whispered.

"That's wassup." He said smiling back at her.

He looked down into his Evo punching through buttons trying to get to the missed call log.

"Wait, you've been glued to that thing all night. Do you want that or do you want me?" Pandora asked hoping she didn't sound like a nagging girlfriend. Even though she hadn't gained that title yet, it sure felt like she owned it.

"You know, you're right babe." Kojack said turning his phone off and throwing it in the back seat. "Now yours."

Pandora hadn't planned on that reaction. The look on her face let him know that she really didn't want to do it. Her phone was mostly used to keep in contact with her sisters just in case they needed her. She took a second to think about the pros and cons before realizing they very rarely needed her for anything. *They're big girls. They can handle their own.* She thought as she took her IPhone out of her pocket staring at it noticing it was on vibrate already. She looked at him side eyed then put her phone to sleep faking as if she had cut it off.

"Done." She said leaning back in the seat, relishing in the sweet summer wind.

Chapter 8- Stained Love

She opened her eyes to a black goateed canvass. It was impeccably painted with sexy thin caramel lips and dreamy sleeping eyes. She took her finger running it across the outer part of his nicely cut lining. He rumbled a bit turning over to let out small bubbles of gas from his backside. Pandora waited with a frown on her face for a smell to seep up from under the 300 thread count sheets that rubbed her body like silk. She was prepared for the foul odor then slowly realized no matter how foul it wasn't enough to make her stay away from him. It could have smelled like the funk of forty thousand years but she knew she would have still been there for him.

Cuddling and spooning with him all night as his bulge pressed against her backside was the hardest thing for her to do. She wanted him to make love to her but she didn't want him to think it was that easy. There was no greater respect that a man had for woman than for her to keep him waiting and she knew that.

Yet, his warm inviting manly essence kept her pulse racing every second. Pandora rolled out of bed cautiously as not to wake him, reaching for her jeans. She dug in her pocket and woke her IPhone noticing she had twenty-five missed calls and they were almost all back-to-back. She glanced over at the time in the corner of the phone; it read 7:45 a.m.

"Damn." She said silently, biting her bottom lip.

She wondered what could have been that important that Lexi had to blow her phone up like that and apart of her felt guilty that she hadn't been there to answer her calls. Slowly creeping up off of the bed, she quickly eased into her clothes and combed her hair with her fingers jaggedly. Kojack was still fast asleep when she slipped on her shoes, snoring lightly like resembling a two-year-old child. His face was so angelic that it made her heart smile ten times over. Pandora looked in his small night table discovering an old light bill and a pen.

This is my new number 773-777-9311. Text me later lover.

Her penmanship was just as beautiful as she as she gazed down upon his lovable face. It pained her to walk out the door and leave him but she knew she had no choice. It was obvious that something was going down at the crib so she knew playtime was over, she needed to get there fast. Her grip on the doorknob was so tight her hand began to throb, hesitant to open it and walk out on the best feeling she had ever known.

Pandora turned back for one last look at her love as she crept out the door without so much as a forehead kiss.

****

"What are you going to do? Call the police? You can't prove a damn thing." The pastor had been yammering on all night about the same shit.

"Shut the fuck up you fucking rapist. You lucky I haven't cut your balls off yet." Diamond spat flicking the ashes from her Newport 100 onto his face.

It was all burned and bruised from the twelve hours of brutal beatings and torture that Lexi and Diamond had given him that it was amazing he was even talking. They tied his hands behind his back to a chair and tied his feet to the bottom of it. His lip was busted and bloody with a few of his teeth lying on the floor. His eyes were almost shut closed from being punched with the thick metal pole Lexi had knocked him unconscious with when she came in. They showed him no mercy breaking ribs and they hoped, breaking kneecaps in the process. Yet, he still pressed on with shit talk.

"You bitches need to read the bible and get into some scripture. You're all whores. That's all you are! The sooner you learn that the...the better off you'll be." The pastor staggered through his words.

He was growing weak and tired from all of the suffering he had endured, dropping his head to his chest. Neither Lexi nor Diamond had any remorse for him.

They watched as he bobbed his head up and down like it was about to fall off. He tried to gain his composure but it was no use. His body was giving up and was on the verge of passing out in dire need of medical attention and rest. Lexi looked down at his wavering body not feeling the least bit of sorrow for him but also not wanting him to die. She knew that kind of scrutiny wouldn't be good for them especially with blood already adorned on their hands.

"Maybe we should just call the cops, Di." Lexi expressed.

"And do what? Let them search the fucking house and find dope and wads of cash upstairs somewhere?" Diamond snapped.

"Shit if we can't find it what makes you think they'll be able to?" Lexi spat rolling her eyes and searching her pocket for a Yomper.

"Cause they the fucking police you fucking idiot!" Diamond snapped again slapping the Yomper out of Lexi's hand. "You need to quit slamming that shit down. It's frying your damn brain."

Lexi smacked her lips and rolled her eyes not feeling like arguing with her. She got up to look for the Yomper behind the couch where it flew. Despite any amount of money they had there was no way she was going to waste a good Yomper. She needed them. They made her feel like she was a cloud in the sky floating as light and as carefree as they were.

They were her home away from home and there was no place like it. Diamond rolled her eyes and shook her head in disgust at her as she walked towards the door looking to see who was jingling the knob.

"Bitch! Where you been?" Diamond snapped pulling Pandora in the door.

"What's all the calls for?" Pandora said ignoring the question.

She walked in the living room to find Lexi laid back off the Yomper she had just taken and the pastor tied to a chair nearly dead. The scene should have shocked the hell out of Pandora but it didn't. She was more concerned with the calls being something more important like the cops were on to them or something to that nature. She dropped and shook her head in disbelief that she raced home for this weak spectacle before her.

"What the fuck happened here?" Pandora asked.

"Yeah while you were out getting your freak on, this motherfucka raped me! For five fucking hours until Lex finally came home and knocked him out." Diamond pointed and muffed him in the head.

"What?" Pandora spat.

"Why you leave us, P?" Lexi asked sounding like a five year old who was about to cry.

"I didn't leave you, boo. I just had some business to take care of." Pandora replied.

"Business? What about us? He could've killed me and you had business to handle?" Diamond felt tears building up in her eyes.

Her feelings were hurt that Pandora wasn't on her A game yesterday. Ever since the incident she had been changing for the worst and it seemed like she showed no signs of going back to her old self. It wasn't like her at all and Diamond wasn't about to let her off that easy. Her teeth grinded so hard it sounded like a jackhammer banging against the concrete and her eye brows seemed to curl all the way over resembling the look of Lucifer himself. Diamond walked over standing toe to toe with Pandora.

"So what you want to do with this fool?" Diamond said showing her gums and teeth sinisterly.

"Shit, let that nigga breathe." Pandora said walking away headed up the stairs.

"What the fuck? What's wrong with you P? I'm not gonna let this nigga live after what he did to me!" Diamond spat.

"Why not? Y'all already beat him senseless. Now y'all even." Pandora retorted.

"Really? Was Sun even when you left him stiff in his house the other night?" Diamond crossed her arms, displaying a sly smirk.

"Tsk, tsk, tsk. Little girls shouldn't play big girl games. Be careful big sis." Pandora said kissing her sister on the cheek then running up the stairs.

Lexi busted out laughing too hard; rolling off the couch and clenching her stomach trying to stop but the giggles had her bad. She looked up pointing at Diamond all in her face with big eyes and her mouth widely stretched rubbing every bit of her treatment in. It was the annoying laugh that Diamond found most intolerable especially in this situation.

"Will you shut up? Damn." Diamond said.

"You are so stupid. You know that?" Lexi said crying laughing as she went to loosen the ropes on the pastor's hands and feet. "You can sit here and dwell on this shit but I'm about to start packing."

Diamond was beyond irate at this point. It was crazy how they were just blowing off what he had done to her like it was a lost football game or something. She wasn't about to just let him get away with the shit she endured and listened to for five hours. She wasn't about to let the things he said about her mother go so easily. There was nothing more she wanted to do than to pop that fool right there on the floor and flee to another country never to think about him again. But Pandora supposedly had a plan and since she was saving their ass right now she didn't want to leave her until she could think of a plan of her own or at least get some money to do so. Diamond watched as the pastor fell to the floor still attached to the chair. His body hit it hard like a dead bag of bones. She kicked him in the face checking to make sure he was still alive and breathing.

"Stupid motherfucka." She spat as she hawked up something nasty and spit it right into his face.

Diamond used the knife from the kitchen counter to cut the rope that bounded his hands and feet. She stood there with the knife in her hand wanting to dig it deep into his pelvis to make him feel what she had felt not only on the night he rapped her but also her whole life in his possession. In her mind, it was time for him to pay for everything he had put her sisters through. The man at her feet was the scum of the fucking earth to her, scum that needed to be scraped and burned never to be seen or heard from again. She gripped the knife tightly creating sweat in her palm trying hard not to let it slip from her fingertips. Her mind drifted back to that night wondering how Pandora stretched Sun out in his bedroom and desiring to do the same right then. She wondered if she had it in her, if she could be the cold hard killer her sister had become.

"Di. You coming, girl?" Lexi asked kneeling down on the steps looking under the top of the corridor.

"Yeah…yeah here I come." Diamond turned slightly making sure not to take her eye off of him just in case he made any sudden moves. "Lucky son of a bitch."

****

"Damn girl! It's hard to believe we've been in here for a whole week. I need to go shake my ass!" Diamond said popping her booty in the air like a video vixen.

"Well you go shake your ass. I got some business to handle in the morning so I'm hitting the sheets." Pandora said turning over and squeezing her pillow firmly.

"Ugh. You are starting to get on my nerve with this shit. And where's Lex?" Diamond spat sassy-like.

"I dunno." Pandora retorted.

They had been living the good life off Sun's dime and his murder was slowly becoming an unsolved mystery. The cops had even begged people to shout a few leads to Crime Stoppers but no good ones came through. Once they were done moving in the first thing Diamond and Pandora did was get driver's licenses so they could get off the bus. They knew they were becoming too important to be without wheels. They were coasting in luxury rental cars, dining at the finest restaurants, shopping, and enjoying the freedom of having a stunning condo overlooking the Chicago scenery. Pandora had spent every day of the last week with Kojack covering up her rendezvous' with the excuse that she was always handling business, figuring out a way for them to make money.

Diamond was so engrossed in her newfound life that she had forgotten about Kojack. She had returned to the hood that night to stunt on the bitches that said they would never make it in life. Not only were they wrong but also they had done it many years before they needed to. She walked down the street romping right through the niggas she used to sleep with and some of the ones she had yet to tap.

Her tight shimmering gold pants coupled with her stylish wedges and black baby tee caught everyone's attention while her thick waist swayed from side to side. She caught Kojack at the end of the crowd spitting game with Tino. He looked in amazement at her attire. He thought it was sexy but Pandora had never dressed like that in front of him when she was pretending to be Diamond. She would always represent him classy and not trashy.

Kojack licked his lips thinking she did that for him and was finally ready to give up the goods. All the time they were kicking it they never had sex. It was more important for him to get to know her inside first before he went in but getting some would definitely be the icing on the cake. She walked right up to Kojack rubbing on his shoulder and mean mugging Tino.

"Oh, so you not gon' say nothin'?" Tino snapped all cocky like.

"Hey." Diamond snapped back with an attitude.

Kojack didn't understand the tension between them but he brushed it off standing in front of Tino to cut off the eye contact. Tino walked off waving his hand pissed off that he did want her first and trying to figure out how the hell Kojack ended up with her. Diamond didn't really have anything against him aside from the rumors that circulated about him. She couldn't have respect for a man who wasn't true to himself about what did. Not to mention he looked liked a snake in the grass and she didn't trust him with a ten-foot pole.

She crossed her eyes then brushed him off feeling like he wasn't even worthy enough to be in her presence.

"What's good babe?" Kojack spat pulling her close and kissing her on the cheek.

"Shit. I was thinking about you so I decided to come through." Diamond spat rubbing up against him like they were at the club.

"Shit I thought we was getting up later, Diamond. I told you I had work to do today." Kojack spat checking the niggas out who was checking her.

"What? I don't remember that. Anyway, I just wanted to show you how good I look. Don't I look like money?" Diamond said turning around like she was on a runway.

Diamond's ass swayed slowly from side to side driving the niggas down street insane. They were all like dogs in heat making howling noises acting like they had never seen ass before. Kojack didn't know where all that shit was coming from but her arrogance was surely pissing him off. He wasn't the type of man to cause a scene or bring drama to himself so he played it as cool as humanly possible. He pulled her towards him leaning in faking like he was kissing her ear.

"I don't know what's going on here but you are embarrassing yourself. I think you need to go home and I will call you later." He whispered.

"What? Am I embarrassing you, Kojack? Oh, Mr. Fine Kojack is so embarrassed by me. Well I don't give a fuck nigga this is who I am." Diamond spat walking away.

He grabbed her arm pulling her back. "Alright.
Maybe that was a little out of line and I see you need some
attention. So let's go."

"Now that's more like it. But we take my car." She
retorted.

"Your car?"

"Yeah nigga my car." She said escorting him back to
her rented Beamer.

Kojack paused. She had never called him that ever
before and instantly knew something was up. He didn't know
if she was playing him shady because she had a little money
or what, but something seemed odd about her. Diamond
noticed his weird looks but paid its no mind. She figured her
confidence was getting to him again but figured all of that
would fly out the windows once she got her mouth on him.
They drove all the way downtown before uttering a word.

"So, you came into some nice money huh?" Kojack
asked.

"Yeah my dad finally gave me my inheritance from
my momma's death." She spat fast.

Diamond pulled up to the Hilton entrance and
hopped out throwing the valet the keys. She grabbed his arm
as they walked into the doors and up to the reservations desk.
The shinning chandeliers and the professionally painted
murals on the wall didn't amuse Kojack. He wasn't impressed
by the rich people walking around with their noses in the air
or by the bellhops lugging luggage up to guest's rooms.

It wasn't that he could not afford it, it was the fact he had no idea why she would bring him to such an elaborate establishment. Diamond paid for the room then was escorted by a bellhop up to it. Once inside she handed the guy a $20 dollar bill and shooed him on his way. He looked at it as if it were a $1 dollar bill, frowning his face up as he slammed the door.

"So, what 'cha think?" Diamond asked looking around the decent room with its huge bed and flat screen TV that hung on the wall adjacent from it.

"It's cool." Kojack replied looking out of the big bay windows at the view. "So what we doing here, Diamond?"

"Nigga, what you think? I wanna see that big ol' thang you workin' with." Diamond said walking to him grabbing the bulge in his pants.

He was limp and even still it had some length on it. She was mesmerized and moist all at the same time from the sight. Her fingers went to unbuckle his pants but were halted by his strong hand. She went for it again but kept getting batted away. Diamond didn't want to get angry and ruin her whole night in the room. She mustered up the strength to be humble and calm before she spoke.

"Damn nigga what's the deal?"

"Shit for starters, you calling me nigga. Where you get that shit from?"

"Oh. You all forceful and junk. I'm sorry daddy. Well let's talk first. So who you been texting all this time?" Diamond said sitting on the floor in front of him.

"Look get in the bed and lay down and don't move. I'm about to go downstairs to that store up the street and get some Yak for us to sip on. When I come back I want the lights off so we can get it in." Kojack spat walking towards the door. "Lights off!"

Kojack went into the lobby slapping hands with the dark figure walking towards him. He didn't feel the least bit guilty about what he was doing. In fact he found it quite amusing. The man fixed his black New York Yankees baseball cap lowering it a little more over his eyes trying not to be seen. Kojack laughed at his poor excuse for hiding but was grateful that he even showed up to help him out in the first place.

"Thanks bro. Room 211. It's open." He said as he shook up with him then walked out the door and headed down the street. He never looked back as he jogged down the stairs of the subway and hopped the "L" back to the hood. Upstairs, the guy pushed door open slowly looking around the room for signs of life. It was pitch black inside leaving him wondering what exactly had Kojack set him up with. He had it in his head that if this chick was a wider than the bed that he was going to run faster than Forest Gump for sure.

"Damn baby that was quick as hell. I'm in the bed waiting baby." Diamond yelled.

The woman's voice sounded to sexy for her to be a Booga Bear and that fact alone enticed him a great deal. The man shut the door quickly then walked around the corner to the bedroom, anxiously undressing on the way. He couldn't wait to get his rocks. When Kojack texted him and told him there was free hot pussy practically throwing it away, he couldn't resist. His nice hard dick beat against the inside of his right leg as he climbed into the bed on top of a naked Diamond. She rubbed his back eager to receive him into her pleasure. She grabbed his firm backside and spread eagle so he could have ample room to maneuver himself in. He put the tip of his head against her opening, gyrating around a bit, teasing, before sticking it in. His dick wasn't long but it was quite thick as he eased into her tight moistness and drove in deep like a power drill.

"AHHH!" Diamond screamed as she tried to run from his heavyweight schlong.

"Naw, don't run now. I got you. I got you."

Diamond recognized that voice whispering in her ear but she was too immersed in the feeling of his massive erection inside of her. It started out rough but began feeling wonderful as she moved her body into his motions. Her moans grew wilder as he tapped her uterus with every stroke pinning her legs up making her feet touch the headboard. She knew Kojack had played her but she didn't care because he had given her what she had yearned for since the pastor raped her. A good piece of dick.

Chapter 9- Slick

The next evening, Pandora hopped out of the red Infinity truck she had rented days before. She walked up to Keisha as she opened the door for her letting her inside. They plopped down on the couch at the same time as Keisha grabbed the remote flicking through channels on the 32" wall mounted flat panel. There was a funny smell in the air that she knew all too well. It used to seep out from under the door of the pastor's bedroom at night long ago.

"What's that smell Kesh?" Pandora asked turning her nose up playing the role.

"Girl, my momma. She been smoking that shit for the last few months cause she says it lessens her pain. It is what it is to me, ya know?" Keisha replied.

"Straight up?" Pandora replied.

"Yep. When she doing that shit, P, I don't even bother her cause I know what she going through. I love her regardless." Keisha spat shaking her head.

Pandora thought about what she had in her pocket. She hadn't come to the hood for nothing and she knew somehow someway she was going to need to pop that shit off.

There was no need for her to hold on to it when there was a gang of money to be had out there. Her palms starting itching when the bright idea exploded in her head.

"Ay, let me holla at your momma for a minute." Pandora said.

Keisha side eyed her as she rose and lead her to the far back room of the bungalow where the smell became more evident. Keisha covered her nose and pointed to the door in the furthest right hand corner.

"Enter at your own risk, P." She said as she darted back to the living room inserting her ass back into the groove she had formed in the couch.

Pandora pushed opened the door, nose uncovered, to find her mother laid back on the bed. There were machines everywhere beeping and ticking. The white bedspread had been ruffled and wreaked of a stench unknown to man. Her tattered silk blue nightgown looked as if she had worn it forever and her hair was wild like she was an animal in a zoo. Empty prescription pill bottles adorned the nightstand, dresser and floor of her room but at least the sun shone brightly through the window shining light on the otherwise dreary scene. It was as if everyday she simply waited for death to take her, not willing to do anything about it.

"What's up baby? I ain't know you still come around here." The older woman said.

Her skin was old and saggy but she was only 45 years old. Pandora went over to sit next to her on the bed and touched her hand, feeling as though she was touching a snake with extra scaly skin. There were empty night train bottles tucked away on the side of the bed. She tried to push them underneath with her foot using the little strength she had but it was no use. She waved them off then placed her body back against the wooden headboard.

"How are you, Ms. Rita?" Pandora asked sincerely.

"Oh, an old bitch like me need to be taken 'round back and shot. Put outta my misery, you know? What's a young thang like you doing back here in all this?" Ms. Rita asked wiping her nose with the back of her hand.

"I just came to check on you, ma'am." Pandora said feeling guilty for the real reason she wanted to speak to her.

"I was born at night but not last night, honey. So what you want? Money? I ain't got no money. We barely paying the mortgage around here as it is and poor Keisha so big won't nobody even hire her ass. I'm broke baby. I can't help you." Ms. Rita spat shaking her head the whole time.

It was a shame that none of her family members would even come around to help her in her time of need. Ms. Rita lived off of her social security and since Keisha couldn't get a job the little scrap they had left barely covered one of their bills. Often times they would make payment arrangements they couldn't keep leaving them in dark or in the cold.

"Naw, Ms. Rita. I don't want nothing from you, I'm good. I wanna help you out for a change." Pandora said pulling the small baggie from out of her pink skimpy shorts pocket.

"Help me? With this? Awe, thank you baby. I really appreciate it, I do."

"Wait now," Pandora said yanking it back before she could snatch it out of her hand, "I need a favor."

"Mmhmm. It's always something. Isn't it?" Ms. Rita snarled.

"No ma'am, not like that. You can have this one bag. Sample it and recommend to your friends. I need customers, Ms. Rita and I wanna set up shop right here so I can have some place safe to do it. Don't trip, I'll do it out of the garage and not out in the open."

Ms. Rita looked into her eyes to figure out what her angle was. She didn't seem like a shiesty person and she was always a respectful girl when she was young.

"So all I get is this one bag?" Ms. Rita asked coyly.

"No ma'am. You can get two bags a day. You need to take it easy cause you're on those meds. But I will also throw Keisha some dough to save for the long run." Pandora retorted.

"Deal. Do what you want. Now hand that over."

Pandora put the bag in her hand then kissed her forehead as she walked out the door. She reached the living room and stood behind the couch staring down at her couch potato friend laughing at reruns of the Jeffersons. The living room was cluttered with old pictures of the good old days when they had no hard times. It was a shrine to her daddy who had been locked down for fifteen years on murder, to when Ms. Rita was young and gorgeous and when Keisha was vibrant and energetic.

"Ay, Keish. Your mom's says I can chill at your crib in the garage from time to time. Where the garage keys?" Pandora said extending her hand.

Keisha asked no questions. She reached into her pocket taking the key off the key ring then handed it to her. Pandora tapped her on the shoulder as she headed out the door hopping back into the truck. She pulled around to the garage, taking out the three bricks of work and storing it underneath some blue tarp in the Far East corner where no one would think to look. Her phone buzzed off the hook when she turned it back on. She had multiple messages come through and a few missed calls. They were all from Kojack.

"Hello?"

"Hey baby. I'm sorry I had my phone off because I was in the hospital visiting my friend's mother. I missed you, though." Pandora said.

"Yeah. You missed me huh? Where you at, Diamond?" He said with the sly tone.

"You know I did. I'm just leaving Holy Cross Hospital. Why you sound different?"

"I need to see you, man, a-sap." Kojack spat with the quickness.

"Um...okay...well where you want to meet?" Pandora replied equivocally.

"I'm at the King Center."

"I'll be there in ten minutes."

Her mind ran rampant as she tried to figure out what was bothering Kojack. His voice was oddly different and strangely peculiar from his usual old self. He wasn't happy or charismatic at all. The inflection in his voice was beyond unpleasant, sounding more like business all the way. She thought he might have been still shook over the Sun shit since none of the niggas in the hood would let it go. It seemed they would work to the death to find his killer.

Pandora bent the corner where the King Center sat and saw that the parking lot wasn't as packed as it usually was for a weekend night. As she pulled in the lot she could see Kojack's car but he was nowhere to be found. She pulled right along side of his car to find him inside with a person she couldn't make out. She exited her car the same time he did reaching out her arms for a hug.

"Hey baby." Pandora said cut short of her hug as Kojack grabbed her arms gently placing them down in front of her.

"Why you lie, Diamond? If that is your real name." He said squinting his eyes looking down into hers.

His tall stature made it impossible for her to look him straight in the eye so because she had to look up at him it seemed as if he was scolding her like she was a four year old. She shook her head playing stupid to his question. Kojack looked furious, though. He meant business and she knew it.

"Lie about what?" She barked.

"What's your real name? Is it Diamond or not?" He asked sarcastically.

She was stuck. No words bled from her mouth because there were none worthy of speaking to him. Her heart contracted fast as she prayed for a distraction, any distraction to get her out of telling him the truth right then. The wind was silent and the night seemed cold even though it was still a simmering summer heat wave. Pandora's palms grew even sweatier than the first day she met him.

She lowered her head in shame and when she lifted it back up to come clean, Diamond popped out of the passenger side of his car with a smile on her face and slamming his car door. She headed over to them twitching her hips the whole way in her sky blue skintight shorts jumper.

Her tits were propped up like she was getting ready to serve them on a sexual platter and the bright red lipstick spread across her lips pissed Pandora off, that was her color.

"Hey lil' sis. Glad you could make it." Diamond spat wrapping her arms under Kojack's.

"What's going on here?" Pandora asked looking at the two of them simultaneously.

"What's going on is you've been pretending to be me this whole time, huh? Tsk, tsk, tsk. You shouldn't be playing big girl games. Isn't that right, Pandora?" Diamond spat laughing hysterically.

"Kojack...I..." Pandora tried to explain.

"Why the fuck you lie? Did you think I wouldn't find out? I'm texting you on the phone thinking you're her when all the time she was in front of me trying to boss me off. How do you think that shit made me feel?" Kojack barked angrily.

"But Kojack if you let me explain..." Pandora begged.

"Naw. You should've been explaining then. You bitches play too many games. Then you always say you want a good man but when you get him you play him. Man, fuck this and fuck y'all." Kojack snapped getting back into his car, screeching his tires as he pulled off.

Pandora wanted to cry but her tears wouldn't fall, not while she was in Diamond's presence. If it weren't for the fact that she was her sister she would've stretched that bitch out right there just like Sun's ass. Diamond stood there with a sly smirk on her face, swinging her arms back and forth waiting on her response to what had just happened. Pandora had none. She began to open the car door but Diamond grabbed her arm. She rolled her eyes turning back uninterested in anything she had to say.

"What, Diamond?"

"Naw, P. Don't get an attitude with me. You need to tell me what the fuck happened."

"For what? He was mine and you fucked that up. Let's just move on." Pandora spat crossing her arms.

"Really? I could've sworn I had him first. That dick was mine, bitch." Diamond rolled her eyes and smacked her lips.

"See, bitch, men are just pieces of ass to you. That's all you care about. But to me he was more than that and I know I was more than that to him. Why the fuck do you think he staged this whole thing? Real men only do that shit for females they care about. Not bitches like you!" Pandora snapped poking her in the shoulder.

"Fuck all that. He was mine and you broke the code. So you will feel shitty when I get him back." Diamond yelled.

"Diamond, you are the dumbest bitch in the world if you think he ever wanted you. You ain't even on his level." Pandora retorted as she laughed getting back into her truck and started pulling off.

"Wait, bitch I took the car back this morning. I need a ride!" Diamond yelled.

"Worthless, pathetic ass bitch." Pandora mumbled.

She had heard Diamond but she didn't care. Her brain was still trying to wrap around the fact that Kojack hated her now. Her heart was heavy and vomit rose in her throat. It couldn't end like that. She wouldn't allow it. What they felt for each other was real and there was no way that fool was getting off that easy.

One way or the other he would have to forgive her for the stupid mistake she made. As she drove out of the parking lot she tried calling his phone but it went straight to voicemail.

You got Jack. You betta hope I hit yo ass back–BEEP.

Chapter 10- No Sister of Mine

Lexi walked in the house the next morning after being missing in action for three days straight. Her hair was in disarray and clothes were wrinkled and filthy like she had been sleeping on the streets the entire time. Pandora and Diamond were not speaking and didn't even speak to her as they watched her plop down at the table and grab some bacon off of Diamond's plate. She looked beat up like she had been to hell and back yet superficially happy. They could tell she was gone off them Yompers again.

"So, what you bitches been up to?" She laughed as Diamond continuously slapped her hand away from her plate.

"Shit." Diamond spat. "Except this bitch stole my man."

"I couldn't steal what you didn't own!" Pandora yelled.

She was sick of Diamond's shit. She picked up her plate launching it at Diamond's head. Diamond stood returning the favor but they both missed each other.

Lexi laughed as she got in between strong-arming both of them. For a high chick that had barely drug herself in the house she was surely full of energy and strength.

"Diamond, I knew the whole time bitch. I saw them leave off the block together one day. You ain't want him anyway bitch, you just wanted to fuck and you know that. Pandora, you was foul, still. Now let's pick this food up and eat, shit." Lexi said attempting to deaden the issue.

"Right, she was foul." Diamond barked.

"So what? You don't deserve him. He's mine and when I get him back I hope you get over yourself." Pandora snapped.

"You ain't getting him back." Diamond retorted.

"Watch me." Pandora barked crossing her arms with a clever grin on her face.

Lexi sat back down picking up the thrown food from off the table and tossing it in her mouth. She didn't even look up at them figuring she had done her job and if they still wanted to kill each other then at least she came home to some action. Diamond hated who Pandora had become in such a short period of time. She didn't know who she was anymore and their close-knit relationship was quickly diminishing.

"I'm outta here." Diamond spat leaving the kitchen.

"Yeah bitch and take your shit with you." Pandora yelled as she headed off to her room slamming the door.

"HA!" Lexi laughed as she continued her meal.

****

"Ay, yo. Can you come get me? I'm on the Cermak/Chinatown Red Line stop." Diamond said.

"Man, who the fuck is this?" Kojack asked clearing his eye boogers to focus in on the time displayed on the alarm clock near his bed. "You better be bleeding 'cause it's 9:07 in the fucking morning."

"It's me…Diamond." She hesitated.

CLICK.

A part of her knew that was coming. She lowered her head knowing that Pandora was right. He never liked her and was all into her sister now. That was the reason why he pulled the old switch on her in the hotel that night. He didn't even respect her enough to just tell her he wasn't interested. It pissed her off that he was the only man she couldn't manipulate into giving her what she wanted. She only had one other person to call and she really didn't want to call him. As her fingers dialed on her IPhone she swallowed her pride clearing the frog from her throat.

"Yo."

"What's good, baby?" Diamond spat playfully.

"Who's this?"

"It's that fire ass pussy from the other night nigga. Now wake your big dick ass up and come swoop a bitch." She spat.

"Where you at?"

She gave him the location then focused in on the
noise in the background. He had had a few bitches in his bed
already and they were all apparently up getting their wake
and bake on. It pained her to even call this nigga knowing
the type of shit he was on but she had no choice. She was
assed out with nowhere to go and she refused to spend the
few hundred dollars she had left in her pocket on some
crummy ass motel room. There was no way she was asking
Pandora for money and she figured Lexi probably blew all of
her money on Yompers.

"Aight, I'll be there in an hour."

"An hour?" She asked worriedly.

"Yeah, I don't stay in the hood baby. Plus I got shit to
handle before you. Just sit tight. A nigga will be there."

She hung up the phone disgusted by his remark. She
had to post up for an hour at a stinky dirty "L" station with
two big duffle bags full of clothes. Homeless people slept on
the benches in the early morning hours and nothing was
open this early on a Saturday, at least nothing close by.
Diamond went downstairs to the street level to the piss-
infested corridor and stacked the two bags on top of each
other and took a seat on them. Passengers gave her the side
eye as they made their way past her to pay for their fares and
go up to the train. They figured she was another homeless
runaway and steered clear of her.

"Ugh." Diamond moaned as an hour passed and there
was still no sign of her ride.

She began to believe he had stood her up. Her bags were beginning to sink down and she was becoming impatient. She snatched up her bags and headed out of the door and down the street. At the end of the block, she was damn near ran over by a red Beamer that had pulled up in front of her blasting some unknown local rap artist. Diamond recognized the car reaching for the door handle but was stopped as the door popped open by itself rising straight up in the air.

"What up shawty?" Tino said, turning the music down.

"You what's up, nigga." She replied as she slid her eager ass in the passenger seat. "Thanks for coming."

"You know my nigga Flex, right?" He asked pointing towards the back seat. "So you homeless girl or what?" He asked checking Flex's reaction to his introduction in the rearview mirror.

Diamond wondered why the hell he had brought him but played it cool knowing she wasn't in the position to make him mad. She desperately needed a place to stay and she was willing to do just about anything to get it. Her feet was hurting from her purple pumps and she was dog tired from not being able to sleep well since the day they left Sun's house so it would be nice to relax at Tino's spot. She nodded her head at Flex acknowledging him and he threw her an eerie sly smile. Diamond smacked her lips then focused her thoughts back on who was important.

"I've seen you at the Center before." Diamond said faking but knowing exactly whom he was from the rumors that had circulated about him and Tino. "Naw, I left my crib and now I wanna bunk with you. Is that cool?" She retorted snotty like.

"Shit that's cool but we need to get a few things straight. One, we ain't together so don't be jocking me when I bring bitches home and two, you ain't about to be lounging doing nothing." He said raising his fingers in the air. "You gots to get up and do something. Cook, clean, or do something, shit."

"I know what I'm supposed to do, nigga." Diamond spat, rolling her eyes and laughing. "But you forgot, you need to be satisfied. So I will fuck you right when the rent is due."

"In that order." He replied as they rode off hopping back on the expressway north to Schaumburg.

Flex seemed to be losing his mind in the back seat from their small conversation. He folded his arms, staring out of the window unable to keep his focus on two anymore. Tino kept his eye on him the whole ride back, not giving in to his bullshit. They arrived at a huge mansion type house that was conveniently down the street from Tino's place. He exited the car waiting for Flex to exit as well then closed the door behind him.

"It was nice meeting you." Diamond yelled out the driver's side window.

Flex and Tino totally ignored her as they walked up to the house's front door. They stood there a minute before speaking looking to see if Diamond was watching them. She was. She watched their every move waiting to see if the rumors about Tino were true. Tino turned around facing Flex as if he wasn't concerned with Diamond's gawking. He didn't want to be the one to speak first but it seemed that flex was so mad he was going to ride out the silence until he couldn't any longer.

"So, what's good?" Tino finally said.

"Shit. You tell me. You got these hoes all up in my face flaunting them and shit like it's nothing. Then you got bitches staying with you. Nigga, you tell me." Flex retorted evilly.

"Man that's nothing. They nothing compared to you." Tino said waving the subject off.

"I can't tell. I mean, how do you think I felt when I'm laid up in your bed and it's bitches on the floor waiting to be fucked by you? I don't get down with no fish so I know they wasn't waiting on me." Flex said with a disheveled look on his face.

"Man, you trippin', man." Tino said as he slowly walked back towards the car.

"Oh yeah. I'm trippin'? Well, would I be trippin' if I told your new little bitch friend about your status?" Flex retorted crossing his arms and twisting his hips.

Tino turned around with the most crazed look on his face. He stared at Flex trying to figure out his angle but not wanting to cause a scene. No one knew his lifestyle outside of his house. He intended to keep I that way but he risked everything playing with Flex's fire. He knew he didn't give a shit about outing a motherfucka since he had claimed to be so in love with Tino. In fact he talked about running away with him and getting married but he knew that would never happen with the type life Tino led.

"You need to slow your role before I hem your ass up real quick." Tino said between his teeth.

"Or what? You ain't gon' do shit wit' yo piss po ass. There's something wrong with what you're doing, Tino. You need to stop before it's too late...I'm mean you know ain't nobody gon' love you like I love you." Flex said with dreamy eyes.

His eyes danced around the subject that he wanted her out of the car and him upstairs in his bed. He had hoped that Tino picked up the hint though. Tino walked back up to him being sure to keep a safe distance. What he was about to say wasn't pretty and he knew a nigga like Flex would pop off at the mouth hard or go crazy trying to bust his balls. He looked off into the distance unwilling to look in the eye.

"I'm done with your ass. Be sick alone."

"What? What? No baby wait. You can't do this! Please!" Flex begged grabbing hold to Tino's hand.

Tino snatched his hand back fast before he could get a decent grip on it. He turned and walked away with the quickness jumping in the car before he went mad. He looked back in his rearview mirror as he started the car for any signs of ignorance on Flex's behalf but all he peeped was he standing there, watching him pull away. He was surprised and actually a little concerned as to why he didn't act a fool like he had originally thought. Tino sat back as he drove of and shrugged his shoulders at the mature way he presented himself when he took the news. He loved the shit out of Flex but his clinginess was out of pocket and uncontrollable. Although, it was one of the sanest breakups he had ever had, he wished he could commend him on that. But he knew it was best to just keep a safe distance, at least for a little while.

****

"Ay, get up." Pandora barked kicking Lexi's footboard.

She walked around to the side of the bed and sat down as Lexi rolled over. Lexi rubbed her eyes and pulled the covers over her head listening but unwilling to fully wake up. Pandora shoved her rocking her back and forth roughly forcing her to to get it together.

"I'm up."

"Now that Diamond's gone it's just me and you lil sis. I love both of you but until she gets it together, I'm done with her." Pandora said.

"We sisters, P." Lexi said sluggishly.

"I don't give a fuck. Now listen, I got this shit going and if you want in to make you some money then I can put you on. You be on the block anyway so I can use your help." Pandora spat.

"Money? What the fuck do I need with money? My big sister supplies everything I need and my friends supply everything I want. Fuck money, but I'll help you 'cause that's what sisters do for each other." Lexi sat up to hug her sister genuinely. "I love you, P."

"I love you back chick. Now let's get this money. Get dressed." Pandora ordered as she slapped Lexi's protruding backside when she turned over trying to get back to sleep. "Give me some of that ass girl. I need a little bit."

"Girl bye. You wouldn't know what to do with all this ass. Ay, ain't you still pure, P?"

"Yeah, I'm pure. But that would've been a distant memory if Di hadn't fucked that up." Pandora replied.

"You was wrong, Pandora. Period. But I don't wanna talk about that shit." Lexi said walking over to her sister grabbing her tits forcefully and licking her lips.

"Bitch, what the fuck are you doing?" Pandora spat pushing her away hard.

"Stop. Just be cool. I just want to see something." Lexi said walking back up to her sliding her fingers in between the crotch part of her yellow mesh booty shorts.

She fingered Pandora's soft clitoris quickly watching as her body trembled and shook profusely. Lexi reached up putting her lips gently to hers then opening her mouth forcing her tongue inside of Pandora's. She oddly reciprocated. She didn't know what the hell was happening but it felt better than when she did it herself.

"Ahh!" Pandora moaned rubbing her nipples to get them nice and hard.

"Pull those titties out bitch. Let me see those big pretty brown nipples." Lexi spat rubbing her mouth against the outside of her shirt.

Lexi was no stranger to sex with girls and had crushes on her twin sisters for the longest. Her fantasies involved Pandora more than Diamond because Pandora was pure, untouched. Diamond got around a lot but she also kept turning Lexi down. She wanted them so badly she could taste their pussies in her sleep but was always too afraid to pursue it.

Yompers gave her courage every time she wanted to do anything else so she seized this opportunity. As she massaged her clit tenderly with her thumb, she attempted to slide her finger inside of Pandora's virginal opening. Pandora opened her eyes from the ecstasy jumping back in fear.

"I can't do that." She muttered silently.

"Girl, let me bust this thang open. You know you want to." Lexi spat sucking one of her pretty brown rounds.

Pandora's pussy tingled worst than a dog in heat. She couldn't get past the feeling long enough to realize the wrong in what was taking place.

"Oh my God. That's so fucking good." Pandora yelled as Lexi sucked her whole left nipple into her mouth easily.

She flickered her tongue back and forth along her dark nipples hardening them, making them point out and salute her. Lexi moved kneeling to the floor pulling her shorts down powerfully and spreading her lips apart, extending her tongue into her sister's clitoral area. She licked all around teasing her clitoris wrongfully making her wait for the main event. The salty fresh skin tasted like butter in her mouth and smelled like lavender as she finally dug into the center of her attention, pulling her lips open even further.

Lexi sucked and pulled on her clitoris like she was sucking on a lollipop. She rubbed her own pussy excitedly while she sucked and licked rapidly on Pandora's pearl tongue, moaning and becoming wet from hearing her scream. She was losing her mind over that young girl's tongue, amazed that she knew what she was doing. She was just like a pro in that aspect and it was definitely proven. Pandora felt weird as the feeling became even more intense.

"I can't take it, Lex. I think I gotta pee." Pandora screamed squeezing her eyes tightly and grabbing the back of her head ramming it further into her pussy. "Oh...oooo!"

"Cum in my mouth bitch!" Lexi said muffled through a mouth full of hot dripping wet snatch.

"Oooo!" Pandora screamed twiddling her nipples faster and faster.

"Mmmmmm!" Lexi moaned sucking up all of her sister's juices. "Did you like that?"

Pandora's legs twitched as she tried to regain her composure attempting to be a grown woman and take the multiple orgasm that Lexi's tongue lashing was giving her. Her tongue showed no signs of stopping as she huffed abundantly squirting juices into her sister's waiting mouth. Finally Pandora was relieved as she rubbed the sweat off of her forehead and leaned against the wall sliding all the way down to the floor.

Her legs were cocked open widely revealing her lightly browned shaved lips. Lexi remained in between her legs sporting a very wide Kool-Aid smile on her face sniffing in all of her loveliness. She stuck her thumb deep in her mouth, sucking it hard and played with her ear with the other. Her satisfaction had been met for the day, feeling calm and relaxed. Pandora, on the other hand, was perplexed by what she had just done staring off at the wall.

"Now you're ready for Kojack. Go get your man, girl." Lexi said slapping Pandora's thick thighs and rolling off of her and onto the floor.

"What the hell just happened?" Pandora asked bafflingly.

"Nothing that you didn't want to happen." Lexi replied.

Pandora sighed still tingling from the previous event. "Did you do this with Di?"

"No. She was cool but she fucks with too many niggas for me to be putting my mouth on her." Lexi retorted.

"Then why me, Lexi?"

"Cause that pussy is pure, untouched, unscathed. It was like forbidden fruit. I just had to taste it."

"That can never happen again, Lex. Do you understand?" Pandora retorted sounding like she was their mother.

Lexi nodded her head in agreement then licked her lips seductively tasting the aftermath. She reached for her jeans pocket and pulled out a Yomper popping it in her mouth and swallowing with no hesitation. Pandora rose without a word and headed into the bathroom to take another shower. The thought of what she had just done with her sister plagued her mind. Instead of thinking about the morality of it she couldn't help but think about how good it felt. She thought about the quick flicker of her tongue and how hot and moist it felt. She had to admit it turned her on to the max and not one ounce of regret surfaced. She giggled as she reminisced about the act and jumped in the shower. Her body was tingling for more but she wanted to save the best for last, Kojack.

Chapter 11- Business As Usual

Diamond rode his face like none other until she finally released. He was too engulfed in his dick being sucked to even focus on not being able to breathe. She busted so hard in his mouth that she caught a Charlie Horse in her leg on the last nut and had to take a small interlude to rub it out. Tino rolled over and posted in between her legs to finish the action she had started, trying to keep her in the mood. Her pussy tasted like bananas to him and he just couldn't get enough. As she continued to rub her leg he planted his tongue deep inside of her opening fucking her like it was his dick. She was shocked at how deep he could go with it as she begun to moan freely.

Tino freed his mouth from her pussy after only a few short licks, rising to stick his fat dick deep inside of her. He raised her legs placing them on his shoulders and locking his arms around her back grabbing her ass. She was hemmed up so tightly that she could barely move or breathe. He positioned himself right above her opening then inserted as roughly as possible but not into her pussy. She bellowed from the top of her lungs while he continued to bash her sweet little backside opening horridly.

"Not so rough." Diamond cried. " Please not so rough."

"Shut up, bitch. Take it." He moaned continuously ramming his piece inside of her.

Diamond cried and begged the whole time feeling her ass being ripped open with every pump. The first time he fucked her in the hotel was nothing like this. He was gentle and banged her like he was making love to her pussy but now he was beating up her tight ass like it had murdered his mother. He was surely taking his frustration out on her snug petite ass. She squeezed her eyes praying he would come soon. Her ass couldn't take any more abuse. Tino felt his dick was God's gift to women. He felt like she should feel privileged that she was even getting a chance to feel him inside of her since there were women veering around the block for a chance at him. She tried to shift her weight so that it wouldn't feel so bad but that was no use. She decided the only way out was to help him get it.

"Yeah, you like this baby. Cum in this ass! My tight sweet little ass. Show it whose boss daddy." Diamond said talking dirty into his ear to egg him on.

Tino listened to her voice admitting that it was soothing in his ear but he wasn't biting. He knew that women often said they wanted a man that lasted for hours but when they got it they grew tired and wanted it to end. But Tino was addicted to Yompers and if he gave up that easily there would be a trick to it. His dick curved slightly to the right so he always broke left when he went deep in.

"Ahh!" Diamond shrieked wanting the show to be over as soon as possible.

She got it. He had proved himself as a man and she would bow down to him at all cost for a roof to remain over her head but he was going to the extreme. He jumped out of her abruptly dripping secretions from his hard junk, lying down then pulling her on top of him. She was thankful that her backside got a rest for a minute but her gratitude would be short lived as he directed his dick to be placed right back into her backside and not her pussy. Diamond felt tears build up in her eyes.

"Please get some lube." She begged as her cries went unanswered.

He shoved her down onto his thick schlong making her take every last bit of it. She bounced up and down on it like she was on a very painful pogo stick. She felt a wet coldness drip from her tight hole and assumed it was blood. It seemed like he would never cum and the act would go on forever. Tino looked down at his dick like it was a prize to be won. He spit down onto her ass cheeks rubbing the spit down onto the hole.

"That's all I'm giving you. That's all you deserve." He recited as he spat again on her ass cheeks and rubbed it in.

Diamond tried to make the best of the situation by rubbing her nipples to cum but the pain trumped everything she tried to do. Diamond tried to cheat and only go halfway down on his dick for a few minutes but that only pissed Tino off even more. He gripped her love handles tightly gradually pushing her down onto his dick then pounding her body against his. Their skin slapped together rapidly enough that those spots began to turn red. Diamond was fed up with being treated like a human garbage disposal. She wasn't about to let him abuse her or her backside any more. She needed a place to stay but she didn't know if she should be sacrificing her dignity to do so.

****

The shop was set up and it was time to go to work. Ms. Rita had loved her sample so much that fiends were lined up around the corner when the garage door opened just to get their fix. Lexi and Keisha was out there handling the business end of things and Pandora stood there for the first day to make sure the operation ran as smoothly as she had planned. All of her business would be word of mouth only and the shop would only be open during certain times of the day. If a fiend wanted that good shit, they had to come during business hours and stock up or go somewhere else. Pandora wasn't about to play that all night shit and risk getting caught up.

"Baby sis, you handle all the money and make sure that shit is correct. I know how much work I got bagged up so don't fuck me." Pandora spat winking one eye at her.

Lexi wanted to slob her down right there in the open but knew it might have freaked some people out. Keisha looked over at their playfulness, laughing it off. She sat at a desk in the corner chopping up and bagging the work and then placed it in a secure lockable drawer. Lexi picked it up as needed only taking out a few at a time. Their operation was slowly becoming a flawless success. Pandora gave them a nod as she walked back in the house and headed straight to Ms. Rita's room. She handed her off her daily package then proceeded to head back out to the girls out back. She secured the .45 behind her back not caring if it was concealed. It was her way of letting everyone know she wasn't for playing any games with them.

Money flowed like water back in the set, as she was thrilled to see her plan coming together. Pandora didn't give a fuck if women came with their babies on their hips or if men came ready to lick some snatch none of that mattered if they didn't have dough. Her game face was on and they better had come with that cheddar, no excuses. She was about her money and would take no shorts from anyone. Her product was just as pure as her pussy with a little potent twist. Her cell didn't ring with Diamond or Kojack's number at all that day, sighing as she slipped it back into her shorts pocket.

"I see you steady checking your phone. If you want him then go get him P." Lexi said shooing her off. "We got you right here."

"I dunno, Lex. This is some serious shit right here. Can you handle it?"

"Bitch, give me the piece and I got this."

Pandora was skeptical about leaving Lexi in charge especially on the first day. Lexi's hotheadedness kept her from thinking rationally sometimes and making sound decisions but she desperately wanted to see Kojack.

"Can you handle the steel?" Pandora asked looking at her with the side eye.

"What you think?" Lexi snapped.

Pandora gave in handing her the piece from behind her back, watching as she stuffed it in her shorts near her pocket. She looked around, checking the scene to make sure it was legit before she left then hopped in the car. Her mind played through the scenario of what might happen when he picked up the phone. She prepared herself for a series of hang-ups but she was going to be relentless so he knew she was real. Her thumb and index finger was posted on the keypad ready to press send. The spit she swallowed felt like a boulder going down her throat as she choked it down and pressed the button.

"What up?" Kojack answered sounding a bit upset.

Pandora could only muster up enough courage to reply, "Hey."

"What up?"

"I thought you wouldn't recognize my voice." She said silently.

"Naw, I know you. I just don't know your real name though." He replied.

"Pandora. My name is Pandora." She spat smiling and nearly cutting him off.

"Ah, Pandora. That's a pretty name." He spat.

"Thanks. Um…I wanted to clear the elephant in the room and hopefully get a chance to plead my case." She retorted.

Kojack was silent. She didn't know what to make of it and it kind of scared her a little. It was hard to read and unbearable to take.

"Well, I guess I'll start. I didn't mean to lie to you. I wanted to tell you so badly but I didn't want you to look at me differently like you're doing now. But Kojack what I feel for you is real." Pandora spat hoping she got through to him.

"Yeah." Kojack retorted seeming uninterested in her attempt to apologize.

"Kojack, I know I lied to you but it was because I needed you. We connected so deeply that I felt like Diamond didn't deserve you."

CLICK!

She was beyond crushed. She thought that her short heart felt speech had touched even the tiniest part of his heart but she was wrong. He still did not want anything to do with her. Pandora pulled herself together reentering her business mode as she angrily exited the car heading back to the set. Lexi turned around checking out her facial expression and already knew what the problem was. It killed her to see her sister so distraught. She took out her cell phone and the business card she had stolen from Diamond and pressed the numbers so fast that she had to take a double take when she was done to make sure she had dialed the right person.

"Hey. We need to talk." She spat on the phone.

"Who is this?"

"You will know in due time. But first thing's first. I need you to meet me tonight." She recited firmly.

"Man, how the fuck you call my phone ordering me around?"

Lexi spat the address and time at him as if she was spitting on the ground. "Be there." She said as she quickly hung up the phone.

"Girl, give me the piece. Let's get money. Fuck niggas." Pandora spat heatedly as she snatched the piece from her sister then walked over to check on Keisha.

Keisha was sweating her ass off under the seriously bright light trying not to inhale any of the smells from the bricks. The facemask she was wearing didn't seem to be helping as she sweltered away in the hot Chicago heat.

"Pandora, why am I the only one doing all the hard work?" Keisha asked pissed off that she was the one that had to chop. "Why can't Lex do this shit? I'm hungry, P."

"Girl, shut the fuck up. You can stand to miss a meal or two with your fat ass. Now keep working cause you are gonna be the first one with your hand out for some money." Pandora snapped.

She was happy to have something to take her mind off of all the bullshit that was going on. There was no sense in sulking over Kojack when there was money to be had and even if she had never won him back she could always fuck her money, spending it left and right. She refused to let her emotions get in the way of her business. Money ruled everything around her. Period.

Chapter 12- Drawn Badly

"What the fuck do you want?" Kojack asked as he jumped out the car and walked up to the red complex building.

"We need to talk. Come with me." Lexi spat, smiling and grabbing his hand gently.

He yanked his hand away, slapping hers down to her side. "You crazy. I ain't going nowhere with you. What's this about?"

"Why does everyone think I will bite them? Look at me. Are you afraid of a poor defenseless little kitten?" She retorted in a playful tone.

She stood closely to his face smelling his manly essence as she gently gripped his hand escorting him into her building and up to their third floor condo. As she turned the key to the door, she flicked on the lights, throwing the keys on the counter and rushing to plop down on their oversized brown leather sofa.

"Come here and sit with me." Lexi suggested as she patted the empty spot on the sofa next to her.

"Man, I'm about to leave if you don't tell me what this is about. The only reason why I came is because I wanted to know whom the fuck you were. But trust that this banger behind my back is itching for some action." Kojack spat leaning on the island counter separating them from the kitchen. "And I'm still waiting to find out. Who the fuck are you?"

"I'm the sugar in your coffee, baby." Lexi retorted alluringly as she walked over to him grabbing a chunk full of the bulge in his slacks.

"Whoa!"

He kept pulling away from Lexi but she was very persistent. She kneeled on the floor in front of him quickly pulling him close to her mouth, breathing heavily.

"Quit fighting me. You know you want it and even if you don't, you'll give me what I want." She spat steady yanking harder and rougher.

She managed to get his zipper undone in the mist of the struggle and dropped his pants to the floor. Her mouth was fixated on securing his limp 9" schlong inside, preparing to suck the skin off of it. Lexi stroked it trying to revive it then looked up at him noticing that he was highly impassive to her advances. He had his arms crossed with his muscles protruding from the creases in his shirt, looking down at her pointless act. Kojack had it his mind set and there was no way she was going to be able to get his dick hard. He had been there and done that before and was a pro at rejection.

Still, Lexi wasn't giving up. She grabbed his dick in her hand and inserted it into her mouth forcefully, sucking as hard as she could yet still remaining gentle. She stroked it using her thumb and index finger to go from the base all the way up to the head while allowing saliva to moisturize the path. Lexi was nasty with it, slurping up the saliva as she bobbed up and down faster and sucking harder. She could feel him gradually growing in her mouth. His dick was warm and smooth going back and forth in her mouth. It wasn't curved or bumpy like most she had dealt with before. It was perfect, like he took excellent care of his dick.

Kojack's head rolled back, pointed towards the ceiling while he struggled to keep his balance. He tried to stay limp but the powerhouse Lexi deemed her mouth was indeed a force to be reckoned with. She slobbed and slurped making loud noises as if she was sopping up a melted ice cream cone from her hand. Her moans were loud and tantalizing sending shock waves through his body. No chick had ever made him cum before just by sucking his dick but it seemed Lexi would be number one today.

"Mmmmmm." Kojack moaned squinting his eyes.

"Fuck my mouth, baby." Lex spat as she pulled his dick out of her mouth and stuffed it back in never skipping a beat.

He was fascinated by this chick's work. Kojack had ran through his fair share of bust downs but never one that could make him bust the way he felt like he would just then. He tried to hold it back but it was no use. She was sucking it out of him and all he could do was grab hold of his shirt and enjoy the ride. The feeling was one so great it needed to be told and sold. He couldn't believe it was actually about to happen for the first time in his entire life. It was coming. He looked down at her to watch the show, peeping what she would do with the nut when it squirted out.

Kojack arched his back preparing for the big bust and at that very moment, Pandora pushed the front door wide open. Kojack looked into her face with shock and disappointment but Lexi was like the Energizer Bunny. She refused to let up until she was satisfied. Kojack couldn't hold it any longer as well releasing all into her mouth letting out the loudest bellow ever heard.

"Ahh, shit!!"

He trembled and shook as he bent over rubbing her back yet trying to break free from her grip. She had swallowed his dick and his seeds without choking allowing it to tap the back of her throat effortlessly.

"Lex! You bitch!" Pandora screamed as she lunged at her.

"Stop it! Calm down!" Lex said firmly grabbing her wrists throwing her down to the floor.

She pinned her down easily but as feisty as Pandora was she could have definitely broken free. It was just too devastating what she had witnessed. Kojack attempted to fix his clothes and get away fucked up by the scene but was halted by Lexi leaning in towards Pandora's face. He could not see exactly what was going on so he moved to the side to get a better view. His eyes didn't prepare him for what they saw leaving him stuck like glue unable to even blink. Lexi mounted her throwing her tongue inside of her mouth, tongue wrestling heavily.

"Damn." Kojack spat feeling his dick growing again.

"Lexi, stop this shit." Pandora pleaded.

"Shut the fuck up. You're so fucking weak, it's sickening." Lexi spat reaching up pulling Kojack's jeans making him fall to the floor.

Kojack stared down into Pandora's eyes feeling there was much more about her that he still didn't know and it was nerve wrecking. Lexi yanked Pandora's shorts down off of her legs and went to work spreading her eagle. Pandora's legs began to shake like an earthquake as Lexi reached over to Kojack's dick stroking it strong and rapidly. Kojack leaned down kissing Pandora's sweet salacious lips passionately. He circled his tongue around hers, grabbing her plumped tits for a brief squeeze then moving his mouth towards them. Pandora was in pure ecstasy feeling double the pleasure traveling all throughout her body.

To her there was confusion and betrayal in the air but at that moment, it did not matter. All that mattered was that her virginity was about to be nonexistent by the man she gave her heart to.

****

Diamond awoke in a pool of her own vomit; feeling like her head had just been beaten in with a two by four. She gazed around the room at the chaotic mess it held. There were two naked women passed out on the floor and empty vodka bottles everywhere. She couldn't even remember what happened the night before but whatever it was she thought it had to have been wild, just like all the other nights. She had only been living with Tino for a few days and already she was swept up into his raunchy, frenzied lifestyle. Her pussy and asshole had been abused ever since she got there and she wanted to leave but quickly came to the realization that doing so would mean she had to go crawling back to her sister. She would rot in hell before she did that.

She tried to rise from the heart shaped massive sized bed but was halted by something stuck in between her legs. The thing was actually hanging out of her asshole and it had a hand attached to it. Diamond tried to remove it but the arm began moving every time she did. She sat up and saw Tino at the foot of the bed snoring like a fucking grizzly bear. He didn't like to cuddle or touch while he was sleeping so he always balled up in a ball making sure no one was near him.

She sat up further trying to remove the object from her ass but the hand began moving slowly forcing it back inside of her.

"What the fuck?" She roared furiously as she opened her legs trying to free herself once more.

Her mouth not only woke everyone up but it angered the female who was fucking her in the ass with the thick purple dildo as she slept. The chick began shoving it into her ass harder displaying an ugly angry mug on her face. Diamond was confused as to her beef with her but whatever it was she was taking it out on her tender little ass.

"Get the fuck off me." Diamond spat scooting away from her in the bed.

"No. I'm not done yet. Come here!" The chick said determinedly.

Diamond forcefully batted the chick's hand away from her legs and slipped off of the dildo flying off of the bed before she could grab her again. The chick sat there with the most sinister expression on her face and started licking the dildo like a dirty lollipop, scaring the shit out of Diamond.

"Nasty bitch." Diamond spat as she grabbed Tino's silk burnt orange robe off the floor and stepped over sex toys as she headed downstairs.

The coffee maker was automatically set to make coffee at a specific time every morning and was now piping fresh and hot. She grabbed a mug from the cupboard and poured herself a cup then sat down. Tino appeared out of nowhere scaring the shit out of her as she jumped spilling drops of boiling hot coffee onto her skin.

"Ah, shit! Damn Tino! Make some fucking noise when you come into the room." She snapped wiping the liquid from her leg with a nearby towel then threw it back on the counter.

"Awe, shut up bitch. Every time I look up you always tripping about something." He retorted.

Diamond rolled her eyes at his shrewd remark. He fixed his self a cup of coffee then slapped her on the ass as he sat down next to her.

"Listen, I'm not complaining. I'm glad to have a place to stay but I can't keep going through this." She spat taking a small sip from her mug.

"Going through what? Sounds like to me you being ungrateful. You're the one that said you would pay me in sex and baby, this is how I get down. You can't hang?" He retorted.

"It has nothing to do with that. I just don't want to do this shit anymore. It's fucking disgusting and my ass hurt from that shit." Diamond spat furiously.

"Bitch do you know who I am? I'm the motherfucking don! Bitches line up around the corner to fuck me. I'm the king and you just the court jester, bitch." Tino said waving his hands in the air crazily.

His loudness sparked the attention of the other bitches in the house and a few filed into the kitchen nosey at what all the fuss was about. Their stomachs growled as they walked in opening the refrigerator and helping themselves to whatever they could find around the house to eat. Tino slammed his mug down on the counter breaking it in a few pieces and spilling its contents onto the floor carelessly. Diamond just sat there quietly shaking her head as he rambled on about how great his existence was to the female race. He felt disrespected in his own house and that thought pissed him off to the third degree.

"Bitch, you can beat it." He spat waving his hand in the air to dismiss her.

Diamond politely got up from the counter leaving her mug behind and walked to the living room. She grabbed a magazine and propped her feet up on the glass coffee table. I'm gon' give that nigga some time to breathe. She thought as she curled and smacked her lips reading about how Amber Rose and Whiz Kalifa were trying to make a baby. Tino walked past her not even realizing she was sitting there. One of the chicks following up behind him like a lost puppy dog spotted her and pointed her out tapping him on the shoulder.

"What the fuck you still doing here?" He snapped as he walked around to her on the couch.

"I'm chillin'. I ain't bothering you." Diamond snapped rolling her eyes and turning up her lips.

"I must be losing my mind." Tino said looking around at the other bitches for validation. "I could've sworn I told you to fucking beat it."

"What?" Diamond said throwing the magazine down, standing up and moving in close to whisper in his ear. "Um…you know I don't have any place to go, Tino."

"That shit ain't my problem. Put your ass to the streets."

Tino grabbed her arm and pushed her towards the front door. His patience was wearing thin with her and her attitude. Tino was rarely nice to people, especially women. When his brother died, he even lost all respect for everyone who was not blood. He grabbed her arm again but Diamond snatched away from his grip refusing to be set out on the street like a pile of garbage.

"NO! You can't just put me out. I got my shit here. I need to get my shit." Diamond demanded.

"What shit? Them dingy ass clothes you brought here. Fuck that! Now get an attitude about that." Tino retorted as he shoved her towards the door again.

"Thanks for nothing you fucking fagot! Yeah I heard you were boss derbing niggas in the 808 building on Halsted. What you think ain't nobody know?" Diamond spat knocking his hands off of her.

His groupies stood there laughing at the whole ordeal. Diamond lunged at them, hitting one smack dead in the jaw as she slipped on the slippery-waxed floor. The girl was heated, signaling for the other girls to help her jump the out numbered Diamond.

"You don't belong in our click anyway ho." One girl screamed as she stomped Diamond's face to a bloody pulp with her colossal sized feet.

When the girls were satisfied with their work they walked away from her leaving nothing but a bloody and gravely beaten mess on the floor. Tino stood over her as if he was looking down on the one who had betrayed him.

"Now get up and get the fuck out of my house." He said as his groupies giggled in the background.

Diamond stood, limping towards the door and coddling her face as it dripped drops of blood all the way to the front door. She wanted to make a break for the stairs to grab at least a few of the things she owned but she feared another beating to her already severely damaged body. She felt her eye begin to swell shut, as the left side of her vision grew dark. Her ribs were recklessly bruised and her stomach felt like it had been doing cartwheels for the last five minutes.

Vomit chunks rose in her throat but she wasn't about to release them and give them another reason to beat the living daylights out of her.

"Oh yeah and one more thing before you go. I got AIDS. BIOTCH!" Tino spat to the laughter of his minions.

Diamond felt her heart drop and her brain explode as her mouth opened in pure utter disbelief. She could not believe what her ears had just been burned with. It was unbelievable that he or anyone would do that to her and never say anything. The bitches in the background were laughing like the shit was cool but he had slept with them too. She could not understand what the big joke was about and why she was the center of it. He rubbed up against their tits and fondled with their smelly pussies as Diamond opened the door about to walk out then collapsed right there in his front doorway.

Chapter 13- Stunned

Lexi stood over the bed watching as Pandora and Kojack lay sleeping like babies. They were none the wiser to her hovering over them, fast asleep from the previous night's events. The past few days had been amazing and she couldn't get either of them out of her mind. In a perfect world, she would marry them both move to their mother's hometown of Jamaica and live happily ever after on Kojack's dime. They seemed like the ultimate trio and she wanted it to last forever. She left the room and headed into the living room to pop a Yomper to get her mind right. Every time she thought of ridiculous things she knew would never happen, she had to diffuse it by self-medicating.

Once the pill had set in she was back down to reality but was dying of hunger. As she stared into the kitchen she realized that nothing would top this morning off better than a full stomach, another Yomper and some great head. She got up and went to work on the stove hooking the bacon up and cracking the eggs open ready to scramble and fry them.

She cranked the music up on her Iphone and plugged the buds in her ears jamming to the sounds of some old school Sade. She had always been told she was an old soul because she never did or acted the way young people her age did.

Meanwhile, in Pandora's room, Kojack was waking up to the sight of Pandora's face. She looked like she was happy and at peace but still there was something about her that he couldn't get around. Ever since the day he caught her in her lie about her identity he hasn't looked at her the same. She was wholeheartedly in the relationship enjoying every minute of it but it seemed he didn't feel the emotion he once did in the beginning. It was hard to trust her since people who start off relationships with lies usually have a ton of other secrets in their closets.

"Hey bay." Pandora said waking to Kojack staring down at her. "How'd you sleep?"

"Well. I slept well." He said searching the nightstand for his cell phone.

"Oh wow. You are always on that thing. Really, Kojack?" Pandora snapped.

"It's my business."

"But your business is with me now. Remember me? Whatever happened to us cutting the phones off when we are togeth—"

"Alright Pandora! Sheesh, you don't have to nag me about it damn." Kojack said frustrated by her speech.

"I didn't know I was nagging you, bay. I'm sorry. It won't happen again." She said turning her head away from him and folding her arms.

Kojack didn't feed into her pouty temper tantrum one bit. He cocked a pillow up and leaned back against the metal headboard. The intoxicating aroma seeped in from under the door tickling their noses and teasing their stomachs. They knew it was Lexi in there cooking some tasty vittles and they hoped she was going to share. Pandora wanted to get up and check it out but she didn't want to give Kojack the satisfaction of having a brief moment to jump on his phone again. She knew once he got on he would never get off. Since he was playing the silent treatment, she was going to give him something to make him feel better.

"Bay, I really am sorry for nagging and to make it up to you, here's a little apology." She said as she disappeared under the covers and in between his legs.

"You know you really don't have to do this, Pandora."

"But I want to baby. Just sit back and relax."

Kojack tried to relax but it was no use. His feathers were already ruffled with displeasure. He tried to close his eyes and concentrate so he could at least get a little bit of action out of the deal but it wouldn't work. She was completely horrible at sucking dick. It was like she only knew how to drive an automatic but was winging driving a stick. She was all over the place with it and at the end of it all his ass was wet from all of the slobber she released not wanting to swallow any spit from the act.

"Why do you even get down there? I mean, do you know what you're doing?" He said grabbing her cheeks, bringing them up for air.

"Of course I do." Pandora lied. "Okay no I don't. I've never done any of this before."

"Any of what before?"

"I've never...I...ugh! Kojack I was a virgin before a few nights ago. You were my first." She said happily smiling ear to ear.

"Ugh...why did you do that Pandora? Why didn't you tell me?" Kojack exclaimed putting his hands on his head.

"Well I didn't think it was something I needed to tell you. It's my choice to give it to who I wanted right? Well I chose you, boo!" She said rubbing his cheek gently.

"Yeah but it would've been nice to have had a choice in the matter." Kojack replied sternly.

"I don't understand what the big deal is here. I gave you something special. You should be fucking grateful that someone like me would even remotely deal with someone like you." She snapped.

"Someone like me?"

Kojack laughed off her remark. He knew she had no idea who the hell she was talking to. She wanted her fifteen minutes of fame so he was letting her swim in that for as long as she wanted to. He had begun to change his mind about her and she wasn't doing anything but making it all the more easy for him to leave her high and dry.

He went silent again leaning back on the bed and not entertaining her ego any longer with bullshit conversation. Pandora sat in disbelief of his actions. He was supposed to be kissing her ass and her feet but he wasn't. Outside of the bedroom door, Lexi had heard every single word they said. She laughed all the way back to the kitchen as she went to go fix their plates.

****

Diamond made groggy incoherent noises as she laid back on the bench trying to come to. Her head was banging hard as she rubbed her eyes attempting to focus and check out her surroundings. The sun beamed brightly in her face slapping her to wake up as well but she couldn't pull it together. She laid back relying on her ears to give her an overall idea of where she was. There were cars passing, birds chirping, and sprinklers going. But she wasn't able to hear people's voices to know whether or not she was alone though there were footsteps.

"Oh my God! Is she dead?" A woman asked walking up to her shielding her young daughter's eyes.

"A dead body mommy? Ooo, can I see?" The little girl exclaimed trying to remove her mother's hands.

"No! Let's get out of here."

The woman walked off quickly before Diamond could put together to words for her. "Help me."

The silence went on for a few more minutes before she had just given up. She sat there in the warm summer's heat hoping to sleep off the headache she was having and wake up refreshed in order to get to safety. It was a long shot but she prayed that if she came to without being raped by a homeless person or worse, she would suck it up and crawl back to Pandora for forgiveness and a place to stay. She was done being hardheaded and stubborn and just wanted to be in her comfort zone again, where everything was safe and she didn't have a care in the world. Besides, what they fell out for was beyond petty especially since Pandora was right.

"Hey young lady. Are ya dead?" A man asked poking at her side.

Diamond wore nothing but short lace slip and Tino's long robe. It barely covered any of her assets and it was open to the public so it was only a matter of time before someone was allured by her voluptuous body and decided to take advantage of her nearly comatose state. The man looked into her eyes, which were rolling all around in her head only displaying the sclera part. It was creepy to the older man but he couldn't take his eyes off of her body. He licked his lips but controlled his urges to grab any part of her.

"Alright we're gonna sit you up here. Okay? You can't be out here like this." The man said lifting her up to a sitting position. "How did you get out here young lady?"

The man began slapping her gently in the face to wake her up. He knew if she drifted off to sleep she may have never woke up. Diamond slightly came to angry that she was receiving small blows to her face. She reached out to the man grabbing hold of his face then feeling up to his hair realizing he had a little to clench. Though her mind was weak her grip was strong as she pulled his head way down attempting to fight him off. She felt violated even though she hadn't been as she raised her other hand up to slap him dead in the face.

"Hey you ain't got to do all that. I'm just trying to help you young lady." The man expressed but Diamond wasn't listening.

"Leave me…alone." She said sluggishly.

"Stop it now. I ain't trying to do nothing girl. I'm trying to help. Are you listening? I only want to help." The man figured if he yelled it in her ear maybe she would listen.

Diamond continued to fight him despite the man's pleas for her to stop. Her swings became more forceful throwing all of the energy she had left into getting this dude away from her. The man couldn't understand why she wasn't accepting his help but he didn't want to take any chances of people riding past assuming the worst. The scene did not look right especially with her unclothed and since she was incoherent it could have easily been mistaken for a rape attempt. It pained the man to see her out there like that because he knew that there weren't many people out there like him, but he had to walk off and leave her.

He wasn't about to go down for some bullshit when he was only trying to be the Good Samaritan. Diamond slumped over letting out a faint moan as nodded her head from left to right.

Time had no meaning as she laid there hunched over on the bench waiting to be able to pull herself together. She nodded drifting in and out of sleep but she tried to remain awake so she could listen out for her surroundings just in case anybody else wanted to try her. But her eyelids grew heavy and her headache was in increasing. It was too much to take in but all she could think about was Tino's words that pierced through her soul. It was like she had been hit with a bolt of lightning that paralyzed her. Then a dark cloud came over her. She could feel it even though she couldn't see it and it didn't appear to be moving along any time soon.

"Ma'am. Ma'am." A man's voice echoed in the distance. "Ma'am, are you okay down there?"

Diamond was still unable to speak clear sentences. Her grogging only confused people more. The man's voice became closer and then there was a sudden stampede of voices. Just hearing them made her head pound harder. She struggled to sit up and open her eyes and was immersed with a ton of hands that were trying to help.

"Oh my God! She looks drugged or something. Somebody call an ambulance." The man said holding her shoulders so she wouldn't fall.

More hands began tugging at her robe desperately trying to cover her and a slew of hands were coddling her and rubbing her head in sympathy.

"Can you hear me?" A woman's voice said in her face.

"Don't worry. Help is on the way." The man's voice said.

He got back on his bus and insisted that everyone get back on with him. He didn't feel that everyone should be all in her face when she was clearly very ill. She could have been contagious but no one cared. They just wanted to be around to help the young lady in need. One of the older guys from the bus decided he was going to pick Diamond up and take her out of the open so she didn't have to continue to be exposed.

"No leave her be. When the police come they will investigate. This might be a crime scene." The bus driver said.

"Yeah unless she's just a young crack head caught up in the life." One of the older heavyset women said curling her lips.

The sound of sirens rung through each ear as the ambulance pulled up, parking crazily. The EMT's jumped out with their equipment and immediately began working on Diamond. The crowd of onlookers had done a good job in the beginning with keeping her awake long enough for help to arrive.

The paramedics had seen it all before so the fact that she wasn't wearing any clothes and was damn near unconscious on a bus stop didn't surprise them one bit. Their voices were calm as if it was just another day at the office for them.

"Does any one of you know this girl?" One of the paramedics asked.

"No. When I stopped here to let a passenger off, she was just sitting here. She looked so young, I just couldn't leave her here." The bus driver replied anxiously.

"Alright sir. We'll take it from here."

They moved her to the gurney and wrapped in a white sheet tightly. After that they quickly started a drip on her and began to move her to the truck. The bus passengers all moved back onto the bus in hopes that the driver would get it moving soon since the show was over. The driver was shaken up having never seen anything like that before and had even called his wife to tell her about what he had discovered on his route.

"Baby, I'm telling you, Jesus must've been watching over her."

Chapter 14- Selfish

"Wakey, wakey. Eggs and bakey." Lexi said holding a tray of breakfast in her hand.

Pandora and Kojack awoke to the smell of eggs, bacon, toast, and fresh smelling orange juice. It was the perfect way to start the day. Kojack kissed her on the forehead then kissed Lexi on the lips feeling like the king of the land with all of the special treatment he had been getting over the past few days. He never wanted to go home. Work was not a factor, since he wasn't ready to leave the glory of it all just yet. Kojack called his business in from his cell the whole time letting his business partners know what inventory to order and what customers to contact. Pandora on the other hand left poor Keisha to fend for herself. She was not in any predicament to take on such a huge operation by herself and they knew it. So it left Lexi and Pandora to go check on their business in shifts.

"Kojack, you are always stuck like glue to that phone. Who the hell do you be texting all day?" Pandora asked taking a bite of her bacon.

Kojack put his phone down realizing he was being rude. "My work."

He was as vague as could be when it came down to what he did. She was always curious as to what he did but he would always say the same thing, construction. It was clear that he was in the dope game but she would have liked to hear him say it. Many drug dealers were in the game and weren't afraid to show it but Kojack was a rare breed, not wanting to reveal too much into his life. The way he conducted business fascinated her because now that she had a little business of her own she figured maybe they could collaborate and get money together.

"Baby, you know you can tell me anything, right?" She spat stroking the side of his face as he shook his head. "So why can't I know what you do for a living."

He turned to her in bewilderment. They had gone through the same question over and over before and she just wouldn't take a simple answer.

"I told you. I'm in construction."

"Kojack that's not a damn answer. I've let it go before but now I just gotta know. What the hell does that mean?" Pandora spat watching as Lexi entered the room plopping down on the bed with her plate of food.

"Ugh. Okay. My dad ran his own construction company when I was little. I loved my dad and wanted to be like him when I grew up. So, when my dad passed away last September, he left the business to me and I've been running it ever since. He trusted me with it cause I went to college got certified and began working right under him right after that to learn the ropes. Now, you know. Happy?" Kojack spat throwing back the rest of his food like he was an animal.

Pandora and Lexi looked at each other in astonishment. They couldn't believe that he was legit. They waited for him to laugh and joke about how he was kidding and explain his dope game but he never did. They were sitting with a made man and didn't even know it. Not only was he a successful business owner but he was also a college graduate. Pandora felt foolish. She had the opportunity to be all those things but she listened to her sister and got mixed up in the wrong things. Now she felt like her life was already fucked and there was no turning back.

"Oh, that's great babe. Congratulations!" Pandora tried to sound sincere but it was dry.

She was clearly jealous of Kojack's success but she was trying to be proud that he was one of the few brothers in the hood who didn't need to sell dope to be on top. She excused herself from the bed, headed for the bathroom and sat on the toilet not releasing any waste. It was a good quiet place to think without disturbance and to collect her thoughts. She tapped her foot on the cold floor repeatedly trying to pull her self together. Why am I bugging? She thought.

The news he just put on them should have been great since he was her man and she could have easily came up off of his dime. But that wasn't good enough for her. She wanted everything he already had, her own business, an education, and a bank full of well earned cash. Her bank account was tight but she desired everything else so badly she could taste it. Right then she decided she would enroll in college for the Fall semester.

Back in the room, Lexi scarfed down her food hungry from the Yomper she had just inhaled. She looked over at Kojack staring down at her. He winked at her then tried to get out of bed but she pounced on him like a cheetah in heat. Without hesitation, she sucked his dick just enough to get it to jump up then she mounted it like it was a horse. She road him rolling her pussy back and forth and rubbing her clit to make the wetness flow down his shaft. Lexi loved the way his dick felt inside of her rubbing her nipples and humping him like a jack rabbit to cum before Pandora came out the bathroom.

"I've always wanted you." She muttered leaning forward so he could suck on her flavorful nipples.

Kojack hadn't heard a word she said, focused on the smoking hot pussy he had on his dick. He hadn't gotten to her because Pandora wanted him all to herself. Lexi knew her sister would never let her have a piece of him so she decided to take it.

"Cum for me baby." She whispered deeply in his ear.

Kojack heard that and it was just the tool he needed to arouse his swimmers. He jerked back feeling himself about to bust but he wasn't ready just yet. Lexi bounced up and down on him rubbing her flat stomach all the way down to her clit. Kojack's temperature rose as he watched her sway seductively on his junk. She was a bonafide pro at what she did, driving him insane.

Pandora was okay but her sex was nothing like the fireworks that happened when he was with Lexi. It was about to happen but he tried to hold it, not wanting it to end. He closed his eyes trying to focus but it was no use, he was cumming and there was nothing that could stop it. Lexi's moans grew louder and louder loving the penetrating motion in her sizzling snatch.

"Oooo, I want more baby. I need more." She whispered.

"Me too baby." Kojack whispered back.

"Cum for me daddy."

He knew it was there. If only she had stopped talking he could have controlled it but there was nothing he could do but release. He wanted to warn her but felt it was best to just throw her off of him. She was on him securely as he grabbed her waist trying to force her off. She rode faster and faster, flicking her clit more and more. The Yompers always made her pussy so wet that she felt like she would burst into a million pieces.

"I wanna cum!" He screamed at the top of her lungs unable to hold it in any longer.

Kojack finally pushed her off of him hoping to have gotten her off in time. She laid on the bed kicking and screaming still rubbing her clit to cum. He kneeled down planting his face in between her legs sucking as hard as he could bobbing his head and fucking her with three fingers inside.

Pandora heard her screams, racing out of the bathroom to find out what the problem was. She watched as Kojack sucked her sister's pussy like none other and Lexi calmed down spewing all of her juices in his mouth. He swallowed and licked all around it like he loved it almost not wanting to stop as she fucked his mouth back with her pussy. Kojack rose licking his lips loving the taste of her youthful snatch in his mouth. It tasted like fresh berries leaving him feeling warm all over. He looked down at Lexi's beautiful pearly white smile, watching as she squirmed in enjoyment over the after affects from his lips.

"Mmmm, thanks baby. I needed that." Lexi said attempting to catch her breath.

"Baby? Bitch, did you take a Yomper?" Pandora bellowed heatedly.

Pandora stopped dead in her tracks glaring down at the scene before her. Lexi gawked at her smiling and shaking her head in assurance. She loved her sister in more ways than one but Kojack was a good fuck and it was not fair that she got to have him all to herself.

She figured if they were all fucking then they should all fuck, no restrictions. Pandora's anger read on her face like an open book. It was dreadful to look in her face so they both just laid in the bed rubbing on each other as if to indicate a job well done.

"Kojack, you know she's only sixteen, right?" Pandora spat.

"Yeah right. Quit playing. Don't no sixteen year old roll her pussy or suck dick like that." Kojack said sarcastically.

"No, it's true. She's my little sister. Tell him, Lex." Pandora retorted.

Lexi put her head down shaking it in shame at the way her sister was behaving. She had done everything that Pandora had wanted her to and still she wasn't satisfied enough to share her wealth. Pandora stood there with a devilish grin on her face crossing her arms in enjoyment. Lexi knew fucking with her would come back to bite her in the ass one day, she just didn't know that day would have came so soon. She looked down in horror at the panic forming in Kojack's voice. If Pandora wasn't her sister she would have dropped her ass right there in the room.

"What? Sixteen? Awe, shit I'm going to jail man!" Kojack snapped rising up from the bed to find his clothes. "And you fucking your little sister?"

"Well technically, she's fucking me cause I've never touched her. She just likes to eat my pussy." Pandora spat happily.

"Wait, Kojack! I'll be seventeen next month. It's only rape if somebody tricks!" Lexi pleaded.

Kojack hadn't heard shit either of them said. He was focused on getting the fuck out of there before anything kicked off. The tension in the air was so thick you couldn't cut it with a chainsaw as Pandora stood there with her arms crossed seemingly happy at the mess she had made. She wasn't about to let another sister come in and ruin what she had finally gotten back.

"I'll call you later, babe." She said as he kissed her on his way out the door.

She tasted the salty pussy leftovers of Lexi on his tongue as he kissed her. She was beyond scorched at the fact that it was in his mouth and now in hers as well.

Lexi sat up on the bed mad as hell at Pandora's cock blocking antic. The look on her face told her that she didn't give a flying fuck what she felt about it either.

"I see how it is. You claim you love us but you only love yourself. I suck your pussy why the fuck can't he suck mine, Pandora." Lexi spat.

Pandora knew she was angry. Lexi had never called her Pandora for anything.

"Because he's mine, Lexi. You knew that. Now fucking me is one thing but he's my man. Mine!" Pandora snapped.

"Bitch, I helped you get him back. And if memory serves me correctly, you stole him from Di. So you didn't even get him fair and square." Lexi spat while her perky tits bounced effortlessly as she got up to find her clothes.

"So what! He's mine now. You're bogus for even trying to fuck him, knowing we're together." Pandora retorted as she got up to hop in the shower.

"You stupid, bitch. You fucked with the wrong one." Lexi mumbled under her breath as she headed for the door but was halted by Maxwell singing on her phone.

"Who this?"

"Is this Alexis Burden?"

"Who wants to know?"

"We have your sister, Diamond Burden in the hospital and she has listed you as next of kin."

"Oh my God! Is she okay? Where is she?"

"She's at Northwest Community Hospital in Shaumburg. Do you know where that is?"

"Yeah bitch I ain't slow. What happened to my sister?"

"Hmph, well, I'll let her tell you when you get here...Bitch!"

Lexi threw her phone back in her pocket figuring she would deal with whoever that was later. She darted to the bathroom pulling the shower curtain back abruptly as she spat to Pandora the conversation she had just had. Pandora seemed unaffected by everything she was saying as she continued to wash her ass.

Lexi wanted to smack the fuck out of her and she would have if she weren't her ride to the hospital. She waited an entire forty-five minutes while Pandora dolled herself and flawlessly fixed her makeup. She tossed her hair much like the white girls do when they play those conceited roles on TV then finally made her debut in the living room.

"Aight. I'm ready." She said grabbing her keys and heading towards the door.

"Skank." Lexi retorted shaking her head in disappointment.

Chapter 15- Blood Brothers

Tino sat in his living room adorned by his bitches watching his favorite show, Love and Hip Hop. It was a marathon and he had missed a few episodes since his brother's death weeks ago so he decided to catch up on them. He sat in his boxers itching away at something in his crotch and coughing up blood heavily. He spat it into a nearby Big Gulp cup filled with the same contents and continued to smoke his blunt laced with coke, a wicked stick. The asshole in him didn't even give two thoughts to Diamond's whereabouts or health. Bitches didn't mean shit to him, especially since he was dying. He figured he shouldn't have to care about anyone who didn't care about him. All they wanted was money and he lingered them around long enough to let them think they were getting it.

None of Tino's friends, however, knew about his condition. He lied to them about it always spinning them off to some other miscellaneous disease like Lupus or Whipple's disease. The females that sat up under him all the time were bitches that were just like him. They all had full blown AIDS and decided they would all take care of each other and fuck each other since the damage was done already.

Tino didn't give a shit about them either. They were there to be his muses, nothing more.

"Get up and go make me a sandwich." He demanded pointing to one of the girls who was sitting on the floor shooting up.

She ignored him, waiting for her dope to kick in.

"Ay! Didn't I say get the fuck up and make me a got damn sandwich?" He barked again.

"I can't daddy, I'm busy." The girl said rocking back and forth.

She couldn't have been much older than Diamond was but her body indicated she had already seen far much more. Her hair was done up in micro braids that he had paid for and she wore a ton of makeup because he told her that she needed to look good around him. But her face made her appear sixty years old and was damn near disfigured from all the beatings Tino delivered before she decided to comply with his every beck and call. She was actually fourteen when she first met Tino who stole her virginity throwing money in her face. He took her on various shopping sprees to Coach and Fendi, places she could not otherwise afford. When her mother took her to the doctor and found out she was four months pregnant with AIDS, she kicked her out on the street never to hear from her again. She had the baby on a filthy bathroom floor of a homeless shelter and left it there to go live with Tino.

"Man you ain't shit but a damn junkie. You 'bout to get your ass out too." Tino said as he snatched his ringing phone from the end table checking the number on the display.

"No daddy. Don't put me out. I'll be good." She said as calmly and quietly as she could.

Tino shook his head in complete and utter repugnance as he looked at the TV's caller ID screen to see who was ringing his house phone off the hook. His eyes rolled in the back of his head as he dreaded answering the phone not wanting to be bothered with bullshit right then. One of the women on the floor looked over at the phone's light blinking on and off wondering if he was waiting on one of them to answer it for him. She reached over to pick it up but kept her eye on Tino the entire time waiting to see if she had his approval. He side eyed her then reached over snatching the phone from the table but by then it had stopped ringing. No less than two seconds later it rang again.

"Yeah, who dis?" Tino asked pretending as if he didn't know, but sounding annoyed.

"What up, baby! Dis Shug."

"Oh. What's da demonstration killa?"

"Man, think I might have the science on your fam's murder. Ya feel me?"

"What? Spit it out nigga!" Tino rose weak and out of breath but interested in his knowledge.

His disease was kicking him in the ass on this day though most days he was okay. He was about to take his pills but he needed to eat first. He grew hungrier and angrier at the chick sitting on the floor high as a kite but too lazy to go fix him some food. Tino began coughing profusely hacking up something awful then sat back down, pointing to one of his older chicks that never gave him any fever about doing shit. She got up at the snap of his fingers and headed to the kitchen.

"You aight, nigga?" Shug said listening to all the commotion in the background.

"What's the info you got?" Tino said cleaning his mouth with his sleeve, ignoring his question.

"Heard it was a set up sting by some bitches, some broads from the hood, Joe. Straight up. I think they working for one of them cats on the block, man, but ain't nobody saying." Shug replied.

He glanced over at his naked informant walking his fingers down to the crack of his ass and sticking one inside. A deep moan engulfed the room as the man scooted over in between Shug's legs and began going to work on his dick, slobbering the whole way down his shaft. Shug signaled for the man to be silent with his craft, as he didn't want to unearth the can of worms he had been hiding. The man giggled hard purposely, wanting Tino to hear his voice. Tino heard it sitting straight up, alert and recognizing the voice instantly. He grew cold in disbelief then slowly became pissed.

"Yeah my dude, them sluts were the last ones with him." Shug continued.

"Some bitches huh? Y'all know who?" Tino spat spitting blood in his cup.

"Naw not yet. But I hear there's some new shit out here all the cluckers on it. It's like that Ether out here nigga." Shug spat.

"Find out fool. Hit me back." Tino retorted roughly.

"I got you nigga. You know I ain't gon' let fam go out like that. That shit was dirty, dog."

Tino wasn't trying to hear all that extra shit Shug kicked at him. He wasn't feeling well and he was ready to get the fuck off the phone so he could get over the sick spell he was in. Shug went on and on about how he loved them and how they were all family but the truth was half the niggas on the block were pissed off that they didn't get to Sun first. There was no telling that if they found the dope and money that they would even give it to Tino. That's just how thirsty most of the niggas in the hood was.

"Yeah…one." Tino said as he hung up in mid-conversation.

Tino was heated. Flex had crossed him and it made his blood boil over ten times. The house became a war zone finding everything wrong with the scenery. He turned his attention back on the junkie sitting in the middle of his floor. She was worthless in his eyes, a waste of space. All she did was flush her life down the drain and pumped what was left of it straight into her arm.

He watched as she rocked and rubbed her arms profusely chanting something no one could understand. Everyone was tired of watching her go through withdrawals and fall in and out of consciousness but no one more than Tino. He despised her more than any one of the other ladies who remained under him. He had no pity for her as she had none for herself.

"Who gave her that shit man?" Tino asked irritably.

No one wanted to fess up. When Tino got mad, beatings ensued and they weren't prepared to deal with that. He looked down at all four of them wondering what was taking them so long to come clean. The cold piece of metal soothing the side of his leg, sitting in between the couch cushions alerted him of its presence, pressing firmly against his leg. He pulled it out pointing it down to them. The older woman came back with a hefty turkey and cheese sandwich with tomatoes that looked like a Panini. It was the only thing that excited him as he took three big chumps of it.

"Delicious. Now that's a bottom bitch." He said bouncing a little from the warm gooey taste in his mouth. "So, who gave her that shit?" He asked again even more pissed off than he was at first and with even less energy.

He pulled his pills out from under the table and popped five of them from different bottles, into his mouth swallowing them with no problem. He looked around at all of them wondering who would fess up first. He reached over rubbing the steel in between the couch as if it were a pet.

The ladies all looked around at each other giving each other the eye to tell before Tino completely lost his mind. Finally, his bottom bitch raised her hand confessing to his question.

"It was me daddy. She kept hounding me for it. So I gave her some of mine." She said taking a seat on the floor.

"You?" He spat.

She shook her head at him, not worried about the consequence. She figured she had just made him happy with the sandwich so she had bought herself a free ticket. Tino stared at her then back at the sandwich. He was in love with it, it seemed as he bounced up and down like a child. Once he had devoured the whole thing he stared down at the empty plate for a few minutes wondering where it had all went. The medicine was kicking in making his appetite return in full force. His stomach ached and growled for more as he thought about licking the crumbs off of the plate.

"You fixed me one sandwich and now it's all gone." Tino barked, snatching the gun from the couch and blasting the woman right between the eyes.

Her body flew back cracking her dome when she hit the floor. The other girls looked in horror at the scene amazed at how fast it had happened. Tino felt a smidgen of his strength coming back. He looked over at the girl still rocking back and forth, talking to herself and unscathed from what had just went down.

She brought her big toe up to her mouth and began sucking on it, loving the salty taste as her wrinkly tits dangled left and right. Without warning and with the quickness, Tino reached up and planted two to her huge forehead as well.

"Now pick this shit up and bury it out back. Six feet bitches." He ordered sitting back on the couch.

He tossed the piece on the glass coffee table in front of him and rolled him up another wicked stick. He wasn't concerned with the other girls and their struggle to clean up the brain matter that had splattered all around the walls and floors or their unwillingness to move and bury two heavy dead bodies. He didn't care about them and he was sure that they didn't care about him. It was all about respect and they would do what they were told so long as they wanted to breathe another day. Tino was only concerned with his own well being because that's who mattered the most.

****

Keisha was rolling in so much dough she didn't know what to do. Pandora or Lexi hadn't stopped by for the day to make the drops like they usually did and business was getting mad hectic over there at the set. She called and called but the both of their phones just kept ringing and going to voicemail. It was a sweltering 98° degrees in that garage and she was tired of being back there by herself. No one was out there helping her to tame the fiends and to decline the shorts with authority.

"What you need?" She spat.

"Give me one." The clucker said quietly.

Keisha handed the small baggie to the smelly dirty young girl as she walked off in a hurry. Left and right cluckers came for their packages. She was tired of being there alone and didn't want to work the set anymore.

She closed the garage door after the last clucker and went in to check on her mother. Ms. Rita was laid back without a care in the world enjoying the frozen air that blew from the old air conditioner posted in her window.

"Ma. Ma, wake up." Keisha said tapping Ms. Rita's toe gently.

"Yeah…what Keish damn!" Ms. Rita snapped waking out of her slumber.

"I closed the set. I'm done." She retorted.

"Oh okay. Pandora closed it for today?" Ms. Rita asked turning over to reposition her sore leg.

"No, I'm shutting this shit down. I don't want to be here by myself without them doing this. What if somebody tries to rob me and shit? It's not safe for us." Keisha spat angrily.

Ms. Rita immediately jumped up gawking at her daughter. She knew her taste everyday would be gone if Keisha didn't work the garage and that simply couldn't happen. Keisha fiddled with her hair and sucked her thumb in an elementary type way. She observed as her mother reached underneath the bed and pulled out an old shoebox, handing it to her.

"Here, you can use this." Ms. Rita said.

Keisha opened the box revealing a long black Glock. She wondered where the hell her mother had gotten this shit. There was no way she was going to use that on anybody, especially since she had no idea how to even use something like that. She had never seen nor held a gun in her life and in truth was deathly afraid of them.

"Ma, I can't take this. I don't even know how to use this." She spat pushing the box away.

"Listen Keish, I ain't gon' be here much longer and you need to think about your future. That money is going to help you when I'm gone." Ms. Rita spat, taking the gun out and showing her how to use it.

"What about your life insurance, ma?"

"That shit ain't much and then you can sell the house for some change but after burying me you probably only gonna have about $3000 in cash left. That ain't enough to take care of you."

"Well, I'll get a job or go back to school, ma. But I ain't gotta do this shit." Keisha spat getting a feel for the gun in her hand realizing how easy it actually was.

"Girl quit being a cry baby now and get your ass out there and make that money. A little extra ain't never hurt nobody and you gon' thank me when Pandora makes you rich. Get on." Ms. Rita spat placing her head back down on the pillow turning away from her daughter's complaints.

Chapter 16- Your Life

"I don't even know why I'm going up her to see this bitch anyway. She don't give a fuck about me so why should I care about her?" Pandora snapped turning the corner and stepping on the gas angrily.

"What do you mean you don't know? Because we're family and family sticks together." Lexi snapped back having had enough of her rude girl attitude.

"So. That's her life. Just like popping Yompers is your life." Pandora retorted.

"Hmph…and being a bitch is your life." Lexi replied mumbling under her breath.

Pandora couldn't deny that she had heard her but she would try to ignore it. She figured she was mostly just salty because of the stunt she pulled with Kojack but she figured she'd be over after a couple of more Yompers. It wasn't like her to be so jealous but she hadn't felt that way before about any other guy and she was damned if she was going to share him without her permission. Besides she was done fucking Lexi anyway. In the back of her mind, that should have never happened.

"Well, if I'm a bitch it's because you bitches made me that way." Pandora said smugly.

"No you became that way when you stuck Sun. What you think that makes you a bad bitch now? No one's scared of you, Pandora."

"I'm not asking for anybody to be afraid of me Alexis. I'm just being me. The me I should've been years ago and then y'all wouldn't be having such a hard time adjusting by now."

"No, P. This ain't you. This is a dumb ass clone of you. This ain't my sister. But you're right, everybody has to live their own lives." Lexi replied turning her head out of the window and folding her arms.

She was done kissing Pandora's ass and catering to her bullshit. There was always a part of her that would love her no matter what because they were family. But the sane part of her was done with Pandora. Lexi side eyed her a number of times before pulling up into the hospital parking lot. She thought about hitting her in the jaw but refrained for fear of drawing too much attention their way. Pandora had a look of apology on her face but she never expressed it. When they exited the car, Lexi walked off ahead of her towards the elevator before Pandora could even speak.

****

Diamond shuffled through the sheets, gawking at all of the gadgets and wires hooked up to her. She looked around noticing that she wasn't in a regular unit of the hospital, and wondered what unit it was. The blood was cleaned from her face but it was still a little swollen and her eye was only slightly shut. She could see the nurse's station was directly across from her room and the unit seemed to go in a circle as she could see the other rooms down and across the hall. There were screams of torture and cries of pain coming from some of the rooms. It began to creep her out as she punched the call button for the nurse.

"Yes." A lady said over the intercom in her room.

"Um, can someone come talk to me about how I got here? I don't know why I'm here." She said as she scooted up in the bed.

"Just sit tight." The lady said hanging up.

The room had all kinds of monitors and machines going, tracking everything her body did. It was like being a caged animal that couldn't break free. Her hair was wild resembling mangy fur. A thin nurse wearing pink scrubs slid her room door open and entered headed straight for the beeping machines without so much as a glance at Diamond. She tugged at cords and pushed buttons checking to make sure they weren't malfunctioning then directed her attention to her patient.

"What ya need darling?" She asked just as cool as can be.

"How the fuck did I get here?" Diamond spat trying to take the needles out of her arms.

"Whoa! No need for the obscenities." The nurse said in a stern tone batting her hands from the needles. "I will tell you what you need to know but respect is key. Now when they found you, you was on a bus stop bench laid out there like you were dead. So when the bus came, the driver called it in and here you are. You're a lucky one."

"Bus stop?" She asked looking puzzled.

The last thing she remembered was Tino talking shit about putting her out his house and then she woke up in a hospital. The nurse had a concerned look on her face like there was more to the story but she did not want to say. Sweat droplets began to form on the nurse's forehead as she tried to ease out of the door to escape the uncomfortable moment. Diamond peeped the look uncertain if she even wanted to know the rest but curiosity killed her.

"What else?" She reluctantly asked.

"Well honey, the doctor will be in shortly to discuss everything with you. Now, I think it's best you hear everything from him." She said as she straightened the sheets on the bed.

"Fuck them sheets! Tell me what's up!" Diamond snapped.

The nurse frowned up and turned cold. She huffed as she stormed out of the room slamming the sliding door behind her. Diamond knew she had fucked up, sitting back in the bed and sighing heavily. She looked out of the huge glass doors at the nurse gawking and talking about her to the other nurses. Her head tilted up towards the ceiling in slow motion hoping that when she came down they would have left her sight. They hadn't. In fact they were staring her down like she they wanted to jump her or worse.

Diamond didn't give a shit about that lady's feelings though, she just needed to know what the fuck was happening to her and when she could leave. Hospitals made her nervous because it seemed as though everyone she loved, checked in alive and checked out dead. She grabbed the nurse's button and the emergency button pressing all of them simultaneously while kicking and screaming.

"Get me the fuck outta here!" She yelled as she knocked over machines she was attached too and rocked the bed from side to side.

They knew she was trying to get attention and wasn't about to feed into her childish antics. The doctor finally politely entered the room with three other patient attendants. They cleaned Diamond's mess then waited for the doctor's orders as he looked through Diamond's paperwork without even batting an eye her way.

He was silent and if it weren't for the sounds of the pages turning she wouldn't have even known there was people in the room. She could see the various looks forming on his face and became increasingly impatient.

"Ms. Burden, I see you're eighteen years old and you are with child. Correct?" The bulky male doctor asked her looking down on her from the out the top of his glasses.

"No doc. You got the wrong chart, fam." Diamond spat, not fazed by his diagnosis.

"Uh, no we've ran many tests on you and you are with child. Looks to me, you're about eight weeks pregnant." The doctor said referring back to his chart.

Diamond's heart dropped in mid-sentence. She didn't know how the hell she got pregnant when she felt fine and felt nothing. Thinking back, she couldn't even figure out whose it could be. Her stomach was as flat as a board as she rubbed it confusingly. At this point, it could've been anybody's bastard child. She shrugged her shoulders knowing that was something she could easily take care of. She didn't like kids nor did she want them so her decision on what to do was already made. The doctor flicked back and forth through papers in his binder. He didn't make eye contact with her as she sucked her teeth and curled her lip.

"Well there's more." The doctor said taking a deep breath and shaking his head in pure disgust. "You've tested positive for the Acquired Immunodeficiency Syndrome disease."

"A what? Fuck all the bullshit doc, just give it to me raw."

"Basically you tested positive for AIDS. You should stop all sexual activity now and talk to everyone you've ever had sex with because they need to get tested. The nurse will be in shortly to give you your walking papers and a few prescriptions for AIDS medications. I suggest you see your regular physician soon to start treatment. " The doctor said emotionless.

"Wait, wait, wait. How could you find out that quickly?" She asked damn near out of breath.

"Excuse me?" The doctor asked with a raised eyebrow.

"I mean…well…I mean a guy I've been sleeping with just told me today that he had AIDS. I've only been sleeping with him for a month. In high school they taught us that it could take 6 weeks to a few years to find out, so how do you know?" Diamond protested.

"We have early detection tests that look for any trace of the disease so people can find out sooner and be able to stop the spread of it." The doctor responded sounding very educated.

"Early…detection."

"Let me ask you a question, Ms. Burden. How long have you been sexually active unprotected?"

"I…um…well…"

With that, the doctor stood patting her on the leg and walked out of the room. She couldn't breathe. It was like the doctor sucked all of the air out of the room when he left. She couldn't feel her toes and her hands were going numb as well. There were always people talking about things like that but once it hit home, it became real. Automatically, she blamed that nasty ass Tino. He was the only one she knew that could've given it to her. She prayed like hell for her sisters not to find out about the tragedy that had became her. While she was praying in they walked with McDonald's in their hands.

"There she is! What the hell was you doing out there girl? What happened to your face?" Lex said as she strolled in dumping the bag right in Diamond's lap.

"Nothing." Diamond said bating away Lexi's nurturing hand. "So you ain't gonna say nothing to me, Pandora?"

"For what? You made your bed and now you lying in it. Right?" Pandora snapped back sassy-like.

Lexi gawked at her in repulsion, rolling her eyes hard and curling her lips then focusing her attention back on her bedridden sister. She rubbed her leg assuring her that everything was okay between the both of them at least. Pandora remained on her high horse refusing to mutter a word as she texted away on her phone.

Diamond smacked her lips and shook her head attempting to ignore all of her sister's stupidity. She grabbed Lexi's hand, giving her a gigantic smile, happy that she was more concerned with her well being than anything else.

"Lex, next time you come and visit me remember to do it alone. Don't bring the bougie princess over there." Diamond spat.

"You know I was wondering what that smell was when I walked in the room and now I know. It's shit. And not just any old shit, no, pure unadulterated dog shit. I'm out Lex." Pandora retorted as she sauntered out of the room.

"Man, I swear I don't know who that bitch is anymore. Straight up." Diamond said shaking her head and feeling tears begin to form eyes.

"I know, girl. I know. I've been thinking the same shit lately. All I care about right now is what's going on with you." Lexi responded.

Diamond wanted to tell her sister all about the conversation she had with the doctor. She wanted to tell her what happened at Tino's house as well but she felt if she had, she would look at her in a whole new light.

This was unfortunately a secret she wouldn't be able to tell anyone and would need to take it to the grave for sure. She looked deeply into her promiscuous sister's eyes and realized she could be in jeopardy as well.

"Lex, I need for you to promise me something."

"Anything, Di. What's up?"

"Promise me you'll go to the doctor for a check up."

"A what? Bitch is you crazy?" Lexi spat laughing her off.

"No, Lex. Straight up. Please for me." Diamond spat sincerely.

"Why is this so important to you, Di?" Lexi asked curiously.

"It just is. Can you do that for me, lil sis?"

"No doubt, Diamond. I'll do it for you." Lexi replied with a pleasant smile.

The two hugged as they changed the subject catching up on old times. Diamond wished she hadn't have ever created the demon that is now Pandora. She knew that one day her antics would come back to bite her in the ass but she didn't know it would be at the cost of losing her sister. Pandora allowed that night to consume and change her into a beast and she loved every minute of it with no regrets. Diamond's eyes bulged into high beams as various thoughts ran through her head about teaching her sister a lesson.

"Alright, hun. Here are your papers and your clothes are in that drawer over there. Now you've got to take these pills as prescribed or else you could have a set back. It's common for people to live longer with this so you can fight–" The nurse said, looking up.

"Um, yeah I got it. Thanks." Diamond interrupted snatching the papers from her hand.

That was the last straw for that nurse. She had never been disrespected like that in her entire career at that hospital and her blistering, aching feet told it. She was already bitter because she was middle aged with no kids and no man and she wasn't about to tolerate some young spoiled heathen with a royal attitude. She wasn't aware of Diamond's plan to keep her mouth shut.

"You know what? If I wasn't saved, I would've been laid your behind out on this floor because you sure do need a whoppin'. Your momma and daddy should've did it and then maybe you wouldn't be in this mess. Learn to keep your legs closed and you wouldn't have this problem." The nurse roared.

"Can you please just shut the fuck up and get out my room so I can leave?" Diamond spat irritably.

"Bitch you need to get on with that shit and leave my sister alone before I get wit' your ass!" Lexi retorted getting in her fighting stance.

"Oh so you okay with your hot to trot sister coming up with that package, huh? You gon' end up just like her then. Curse at that!" The nurse said as she strutted out the door.

Lexi slowly turned to Diamond trying to see what her face read. If she was holding a secret, Diamond wouldn't be able to keep it, not from her. She avoided eye contact with Lexi obviously. She didn't want to look into her eyes and tell her a bold face lie but she would if it came down to it.

She slipped her clothes on in a millisecond then bagged up the rest of her belongings and signed out of the hospital. Lexi wouldn't let up on the inquisitive look that she stared her down with. As they crossed the street haling a cab, Lexi couldn't wait for her to offer up the information any longer.

"What up?" Diamond asked tired of her eyes burning a hole in her face.

"You know." Lexi replied.

"Ugh, it's nothing Lex. Let it go."

"Is this the same nothing that you want me to go get checked out for?" Lexi asked.

"Maybe."

"No! Stop and tell me what the fuck is going on! Are you pregnant?" Lexi spat grabbing her sister's arm aggressively.

Diamond was surprised that she didn't automatically assume something worse. It made her smile a little inside knowing that. She grabbed Lexi by the back of the neck squeezing and shaking her a tad.

"Yes, Lex. I'm pregnant." Diamond laughed.

"Really? Oh my God! I'm gonna be an aunt!" Lexi danced.

"No you're not cause I'm getting an abortion." Diamond spat with the stink face. "Meanwhile, we got bigger fish to fry. We need to hit the bank real quick."

"The bank, Di? For what?"

"I've gotta see a dog about an old bone."

Chapter 17- Bad Bitch

All that could be heard from the back of Pandora's truck were her sensual moans of lust. She was thrilled to have her man back and to have also had him break her virginity. He was now officially her one and only true love. She knew that their love would last a lifetime because she hadn't yearned for anyone else the way she had for him. The little sexcapade that happened between him, her, and Lexi was a distant memory and she would make sure of it by sexing him crazy. He would be too busy to want anything else.

"Ugh! Pandora, you are trying to hard baby. Stop forcing it." Kojack spat.

"Okay like this baby?" She asked.

"No. Just go up and down slowly."

"Like this?"

"No. No. Let's just forget it." Kojack retorted.

"Okay." Pandora happily jumped up wiping her mouth. "So, you ready to do me now?"

"Girl. I ain't even in the mood anymore."

"Why not? You didn't seem to have a problem when Lex was sucking your dick." Pandora snapped.

Kojack daydreamed about Lexi. He found himself unable to speak when he heard her name knowing that she was the shit in every way imaginable but long term untouchable. If she were just a few years older he would have dropped Pandora's needy ass for Lexi. Even though he was back with her it just didn't feel the same as before. The spark was missing. It was gone. They were merely fucking to keep them connected but Kojack could not get it together.

"Ay, hit me later. I got some business to take care of." Kojack said pulling up his pants.

"But what about my needs?" She fussed.

"I don't know what to tell you. I gotta go." He said pissed that his balls were hurting.

He wanted to cum so badly but there was virtually nothing he could do about it but jag off or go find him a bust-down. He was not interested in either since both came with consequences so he decided he would just go home to a cold shower and some old school shows of WWF wrestling. Pandora was not working for him especially after the shit he's been through with her in the short time they had been together. The whole thing was messy which was something that he just wasn't used to. He buckled his pants then climbed back into the driver's seat checking his mirrors for onlookers. He waited for a few seconds before becoming bored with her lingering around for him to change his mind.

"You ready?" He asked annoyed.

"Yeah, ready to get my pussy licked." She responded.

"Well, you short on that."

His words cut through her soul like razor blades on onions. She hopped out of his car and into hers without so much as a valediction and slamming his door. She stood outside of his car for a minute waiting to see if he would run after her. It was all she wanted him to do, beg for her to forgive him and plead to get in between her legs. She would have loved for him to gravel at her feet but as his car tires screeched away from her with the car vanishing out of sight she knew that was far from happening. Her cell phone wasn't positioned right in her pocket digging a whole in her side. She removed it and checked out the display, which showed multiple missed calls from various people, but only a few were important to her at that point.

"Yeah, Keisha."

"Look, y'all are bogus for leaving me here like this. I need for somebody to get here and help me. I'm ain't sign up to do this shit by myself, P." Keisha snapped rambling on.

"Alright, alright. Pipe down. I'll be there in a minute."

****

"Just follow my lead." Diamond whispered quietly.

She walked up to the counter with her properly filled out slip and handed it to the teller. Her nerves were on edge but she was maintaining perfectly, looking confidently solid. She flicked her hair and tugged down her purple shimmering cocktail dress that she had borrowed from Lexi.

Of course it was a little big in the butt part but she still filled it out pretty well.

"Um, so ma'am you want to withdraw the entire amount. May I ask why?" The teller asked suspecting.

"Yes. I'm switching my primary bank and I would like to get all of my money. Thanks." Diamond said as poised as could be.

"Okay. Let me just check with the manager." The teller walked off to a gray haired old white man in the back of the office. He peeked his head out of his door to catch a small glimpse of Diamond then headed straight for them. He rubbed his head profusely seemingly nervous about approaching the window.

"Can I help you?" He muttered.

"Hi, Bill. Yes you can. I would like to withdraw all of my money please." She answered.

Bill looked around the room at his employees and shooed them off letting them know he had the situation under control. He turned back to Diamond with the most sinister look on his face.

"What the hell are you doing here at my place of business, Diamond? You trying to get me fired or something?" Bill's tone of voice was hostile.

"Oh no, Bill. This is not a personal vendetta against you or nothing. I just need that got damn money. Now Bill." She demanded.

"Well I'm sorry I just can't got damn give it to you."
He replied as his protruding beer belly jumped up and down
and his country accent began to emerge.

"Oh really. Well I would hate to call Marsha and tell
her that all of those sleepless nights she went through were
because you were laid up with little old me. Oops!" Diamond
exclaimed covering her mouth shyly. "Do I still have her
number in my Iphone? Oh, I think I do."

"You fucking wouldn't!"

"I fucking would Bill. Now I think you ought to play
ball with me cause you know yours are right in the palm of
my hands. Do I need to squeeze?" Diamond said smiling
brightly.

"Got damn it! What do you want from me gal?" Bill
said looking for the head boss.

"I just need you to authorize that tiny sheet of paper
that says I can walk out of here with $50,000 and we're all
good baby."

Bill rubbed his head profusely as he wrote his name
on the paper and walked to the back to hand it to the teller.
The stunned look on her face was priceless as she walked
back to the desk. She wiped the look off of her face before
she got there not wanting to cause a scene then typed some
things on the her computer. Bill stood in the corner watchi
the whole procedure in horror. If someone found out abou
this and it came back to him he would be beyond fired. He
lowered his head with every keystroke the teller made.

"How would you like this back ma'am?" The teller asked typing waiting on her to respond.

"Uh, hundreds please. Yes, that'll work and you can fill it in this suitcase. Thank you!" Diamond spat enthusiastically.

The woman pointed to the glass door at the end of the counter and opened it taking the silver suitcase from her then disappearing into the back room for a few minutes. Lexi glanced at Diamond with her sly smirk amazed at the kind of connects she had. Her sister had everyone man she had sex with in her back pocket and they were willing to do whatever they needed to in order to keep her quiet. The teller peeked her head around the corner of the back room then returned with the suitcase closed tightly. She signaled to Diamond to meet her back at the glass door as she reluctantly handed the filled heavy suitcase to Diamond then hurried to close the door back. The woman signaled for her to go back to her window to finish the transaction.

"Is there anything else I can do for you?" The teller said displaying a fake grin.

"No, but...Ay, Bill!" Diamond yelled, as she knocked hard on the thick paned glass. "You might wanna go to the doctor and get checked out. You might be burning!"

She and Lexi laughed hysterically on their way out of the door. Scheming was one of the many things they liked doing together. It felt good to be back with her favorite sister doing what they knew how to do best.

Diamond wanted to tell her sister so badly that she might not have that long to live especially since she knew she wouldn't be able to take those pills for very long. She hated taking pills that much that she was willing to risk her life to elude taking them.

****

Keisha side eyed every corner of the alley. It was weird but it felt like something or someone was watching her like a hawk. She could feel them but she couldn't see them. It tore her up inside, wanting to yell for them to come out and show themselves but not knowing if she was just delusional.

She jumped breathing heavily as a three weird taps graced her shoulder. She put her dukes up ready to box a motherfucker if they tried anything funny but the truth was that bitch was scared out of her mind.

"Fuck you jumping for?" Pandora asked laughing in her face.

"Bitch 'cause you trippin'. How you just gon' leave me here by myself?" Keisha said wiping the sweat off her forehead and handing her the wad of bills from her bra.

"Awe, your scary ass. What's the worst that could happen? You get robbed. Anyway, how's Ms. Rita doing?" Pandora questioned snatching the cash from her hands playfully counting every single bill.

"She's in her room passed out thanks to your shit. I don't like seeing my momma that way everyday all day, P. It ain't cool and I for damn sure don't like working the set by myself. I quit." Kesiha spat throwing down the baggies in her hand.

"Tramp, you can't quit 'til I tell you to." Pandora snapped.

"Oh yeah, bitch? Watch me." Keisha began to walk off.

Cluckers walked on the scene ready to purchase product. They sniffed out the bags on the ground and went to reach for them swiftly before anyone saw them.

Pandora reached behind her back and pulled out her instrument ready to pump a few into their heads. The held their hands up and backed up smiling not wanting any trouble.

"I never leave home without it baby. Now fucking wait." She told them as they eased back behind the garage opening.

She turned quickly pointing the piece at Keisha. "Hey ho! I said you can't go!"

Keisha turned around staring at the long barrel pointed in front of her. Her palms became sweaty and her knees became weak but not for her, for her mother. When she remembered her mother she thought of the wisdom she had given her a few days ago and pulled it out pointing back at Pandora.

"What you think you the only one that carry one of those? Huh, bitch?" Kesiha said biting her bottom lip.

"Keish, you don't wanna do this man." Pandora eased her finger up and down the trigger caressing it slowly.

"Naw, you don't want to do this lil homie. I thought we was cool but I guess not. You ain't the same bitch and for that I can't fuck with you no more." Keisha said waving the gun. "Now I think it's best if you take your product and leave."

"KEISHA!" Ms. Rita yelled using all of her strength. "What's going on back there?"

"Nothing ma! Pandora was just leaving." She answered.

"Naw. Tell her to come here for a second." Ms. Rita retorted.

Pandora walked past Keisha bumping into her shoulder hard almost knocking her into the wall. Keisha rolled her eyes then went to pick up the baggies and exchanged them for the money the cluckers had. They were short and Pandora didn't like that but Keisha let them slide anyway. Dumb trick. She thought as she shook her head and rolled her eyes.

Back in Ms. Rita's room, Pandora flopped down on her bed inhaling all the smoke of her cigarette yearning for a taste. She reached over putting her hand out for the one in her hand, but Ms. Rita jerked back not wanting to give her any.

She took one finger from her cigarette hand and pointed down to the box full of them urging her to get her own. Pandora grabbed it opening the lid and snatching out a long Newport. She put it to her lips then swooped up the lighter flicking it with one sift of her thumb taking a long drag. She wasn't really a smoker, but when she was in the presence of the smoke it called to her every time.

"What's good Ms. Rita?" Pandora said throwing the lighter back down on the stand.

"Listen. My girl don't like to be out there by herself now. I thought you were going to have someone back there with her. What's goin' on?" Ms. Rita said with a raised eyebrow.

"Look, I'm not about to baby this bitch. If she can't handle the set then I'm gon' move it. Simple as that. But that means your little daily sample will be gone too." Pandora snapped.

"Don't get sassy with me, trick. I'm just saying my daughter needs somebody back there with her. You said you would handle the business, so handle it." Ms. Rita snapped back.

"Before I came here, you was nickeling and diming with this bullshit cut from around the way. I bless you with this good drop and now you buzzin' at me, Rita?"

"See that's what's wrong with you little young hoes. You bitches don't know your asses from your little nasty pussies. Gon' out there and do what you do but I'll tell you this, if my only child gets caught up and you ain't there, somebody's ass is on the line."

Pandora looked deep into Ms. Rita's eyes and knew she was not playing. It boiled her soul to have this old bat talk to her that way but her scare tactic wasn't scary enough.

"Her blood is on your hands, Rita."

Chapter 18- Not Me

Diamond turned the key to the luxurious Waldorf Astoria king suite. Lexi looked around the room in awe at all of the shiny tables and lamps that adorned the room. There was a 42" black LCD TV tucked away inside of its own hideaway in the wall above the electric fireplace. The elegant room amazed them both containing a refrigerator in one corner and a neatly made king sized bed in another. It was just the perfect getaway they needed. Diamond had paid for the whole week but was already thinking about paying for another. She cared less about the money it didn't matter to her. It was time for her to live life and she was going to do so before time ran out.

"So what we gon' do with all this money, Di?" Lexi spat falling into the plush sofa sitting in front of the fireplace.

"Little sis, there is nothing else to do with it…BUT SPEND IT!" Diamond shouted raising her arms high then leaping backwards on the oversized bed.

The two laughed as they thought more on what they should do first. Lexi's mind was running a mile a minute with ideas when she was distracted by the vibrating sensation in her jeans pocket.

She dreaded looking at it since she already knew whom it was.

Her eyes rolled to the back of her and when they came back around she stared dead into the display at the name she didn't want to see. Pandora. The vibrating stopped them abruptly started again revealing the same person on the display. Lexi threw it against the couch getting up with the shit face.

"What's wrong with you?" Diamond asked noticing her unpleasant disposition.

"It's your damn sister. I swear I don't feel like talking to her right now." Lexi said plopping down next to her on the bed.

"Well, shit don't. Nobody is forcing you to work with that bitch. Fuck her." Diamond said stroking her sister's bob.

Diamond wasn't really Lexi's type but she was fiending for some action and was ready to get it in. She reached into her pocket pulling out a bag of Yompers of all different colors. She had red with a moon on top and purple with a lion printed on it. The ones she liked most and that gave her the most kick were the yellow ones with tigers on them. She took one of those out the bag and popped it in her mouth then stuffed it back down in her pocket. Her hand began to have a mind of it's own as she reached over to rub on Diamond's tits as they pointed straight up into the air. Diamond batted her hand away with the quickness.

"Lex, now I love you to shit but I told you last time, I ain't on that with you. We did that shit that one time in front of Sun but that was it." Diamond spat sternly.

"Awe, com' on. It ain't gon' hurt. Shit we blood. You know what I got and I know what you got." Lexi said extending her tongue out over Diamond's shirt where her nipple would be.

"Girl, don't make me hit you in the face, now. No! Your nasty ass." Diamond rose laughing headed towards the bathroom.

Diamond locked the door, turned on the shower as hot as can be and lowered the toilet seat. She sat down with tears as large as an ocean falling from her eyes. Her mouth was wide open but no sound eroded from it. She just wanted to find a razor blade and kill herself before the ailing disease had a chance to. If she was going to go it would be on her terms. Knock! Knock! Knock! Diamond knew she wanted to talk but she wasn't in the mood. Lexi didn't realize her rejecting her had nothing to do with her.

"Com' on Di, answer me. I didn't mean to freak you out. I'm sorry." Lexi yelled through the door.

"Naw, I'm good. Ay, why don't you take some cash and beat it. I need some time alone right now." Diamond yelled trying not to let the sound of crying seep through.

Lexi hated it when she said that. It always made her feel like she was the little girl all over again, who got left in the house all the time because she was too young to go anywhere. It was a feeling she could do without since Diamond seemed like the only person she had left. Leaving didn't seem like a bad idea since she was out of Yompers and in dire need of some loving affection. She knew that she wasn't going to be able to get either sitting in a hotel room up under a sulking Diamond but she had no clue as to what she wanted to get into.

She wasn't in the mood for Pandora's selfishness and there was no way she would end up at the house with the pastor. Lexi took her cell out and stared at it for a few seconds then dialed the first number that came to mind. It may have been the wrong number to dial in her mind and it was definitely a long shot but she knew she had to find something to get into before she lost her mind. Her veins began to feel like fire from being sober for so long so she needed to get to a Yomper fast.

"Hello?" The voice said on the other end of the line.

Lexi was in dire need, alright, of some good sex and a good kick and she knew just where to get them both.

****

"Why you can't call nobody?" Pandora spat as she drove down King Drive headed back to the crib.

"Girl, yo' ass is trippin' for real. Didn't I just fuck with you no less than ten hours ago?" Kojack spat angrily.

"Yeah but it's been all day and you ain't called me yet. What's going on, Kojack?" She asked sweetly.

"You need to find a job or go to school or something cause you too fixated on me, man." Kojack responded.

"Oh baby, I got a job. Trust that. Where you think I've been all day?" She said smiling.

"Oh yeah. Where?"

"Uh, um…Shark's Fish on 63rd and Francisco."

"Come on now, Pandora. You too high maintenance to be working in some shit like that. You really expect me to believe that?"

"It's true Kojack. I needed some money so they hired me."

"There you go lying again. I'm out Pandora."

Click.

"Kojack! Uggghhh!" Pandora screamed as she threw her phone against the passenger side window.

She was tired of him hanging up on her and she was tired of chasing after him. He's the man, he should be chasing after me. She thought wondering what made him better than her. She shook her head then exited the car headed toward the elevator. Oddly enough, the button was already lit bright red as she stood in the parking garage waiting for the doors to open. Pandora watched as the elevator doors opened, stepping in and pressing her floor, leaning against the wall in pure distress.

The elevator doors buckled and opened once more as if they were stopped by force but nothing was there. She looked around to see if someone was trying to board it but the garage was empty.

The doors closed then buckled again. Pandora was already aggravated and that did nothing but aggravate her even more. She walked out of the elevator headed towards the stairs as a hand reached around her mouth pulling her back into the darkness. She almost pissed on her self not knowing who was behind her or what they wanted. She felt her piece being ripped from behind her back out of her shorts. Screaming was useless and resistance was futile because the beast holding her was an amazon at best. The only thing she could feel was strong broad arms and boats for fingers. He released her pushing her into a corner where the garage lights didn't shine.

"Diamond Burden. You've been a naughty girl. You've stolen something that doesn't belong to you and if you don't return it in forty eight hours, you're a dead bitch." The tall bulky figure said in a deep raspy voice.

"I'm not Diamond. You got me fucked up dude. I don't have shit of yours." Pandora spat sassy-like trying to walk towards him to get a better view.

"You don't seem to understand." He said holding his hand up pushing her back into the darkness. "You stole something that doesn't belong to you. You've got until Friday at midnight."

The figure flicked a business card at her then walked away disappearing into the night just as quickly as he came. Pandora let out a huge sigh of relief but it was short lived as she realized he took the gun she had stolen from Sun. If he didn't look at the gun recognizing it then once he did he would definitely know the truth as soon as he did.

"Damn!" She breathed, picking up the card staring down at the seven digits written on the card.

Pandora skipped the elevator and scurried up the stairs to her condo, opening it quickly and double locking the door. She was nervous wondering whom that dude was and how he had found her. Though the feeling set in that it was only a matter of time before someone retaliated and avenged Sun's death, she wasn't prepared to give anything up so quickly. She went to the bathroom and ran the cold water throwing a little bit of it on her face and in her mouth. Whoever he was he wanted Diamond, not her. *Shit, if he wants her he can have her. Better her than me.* She thought.

****

"Lexi you bogus as hell boo. You come and fuck whenever you want then I don't hear from you for another six months. What's the deal?" The young sounding Brandi said taking a small drag of her cigarette.

"Shut the fuck up. Damn. I come get this pussy when I'm ready and you either gon' give it to me or you not. Simple." Lexi spat sounding like an old school player.

The woman pouted not liking to be treated like some sort of whore but Lexi had that fire head and she just couldn't give it up. Lexi had been screwing around with her for a year but their relationship had been anything but picture perfect. Lexi used to have class with her then fifteen-year-old daughter but once she found out Lexi had seduced her mother, she moved out and went to go live with her grandmother, unable to see them together. Brandi didn't care about the fact that she was married to a CTA bus driver with six kids as long as she supplied that fire tongue she was boss in her book. Lexi could have told her to go to the end of the moon and back, she would have did it all so she could get tasted once more.

"You need some money this time baby?"

"Naw. Just give me like a sack of Yompers and we straight." Lexi said pointing to the drawer where Brandi kept her stash.

Brandi kept Yompers in hefty loads because she popped them more heavily than Lexi did. She needed them morning, noon, and night and every hour in between. There wasn't a chance that she would ever let her high go down because if she did the manic depression that she suffered from would only get worse. Lexi had caught her one time with her kids all naked and sitting in the tub with a shotgun.

She was ready to end it all right then and there. The kids were crying hysterically half traumatized by the scene and if it wasn't for Lexi coming over to get some sex, it would have been a gory incident for the nightly news to report.

"I could go re-up on more Yompers for you, baby."

"Naw, I'm good, Brandi. You doin' too much. Just keep that pussy nice and tight so it's right every time I come. You hear?" Lexi retorted.

"Yes, baby." Brandi responded giving her the healthiest tongue-lashing to her mouth she had ever given her.

Lexi didn't normally like to kiss but she was all for the shit on this day being horny as hell and unable to get whom she really wanted. Kojack. As she slid her shirt off, working her way down to her jeans her cell phone began to vibrate crazily. She ignored it already knowing who it was. Her attention was more fixated on preparing her self for another round with Brandi. She popped another Yomper then grabbed her cigarette taking a few pulls before putting it out in the ashtray aside the bed. She leaned into her groping her soft tits like a high school boy in heat. She moved her lips down to them ready to suck on her small lightly brown nipples as she listened to Brandi's kids play loudly in the hallway.

BANG!

"What the fuck is going on in here?" A short stocky man yelled kicking the door in.

The kids, who ranged in ages from four to eleven, were all gathered behind their daddy to watch the show. *Shit!* Lexi thought as she began to regret her decision of coming over there in the first place. She very rarely went to Brandi's but her horniness got the best of her. She jumped up startled by the man's loud voice. The man had a small stature resembling that of Webster, but his bark was very loud. Lexi had never had a run in with him before and wondered how she had been caught slipping this time. She wasn't in the mood to argue especially over a chick she really didn't care for.

"Ugh, look, if you want to join in so we all can have some fun, I ain't got a problem with that, ya know." Lexi said as calm as could be, rolling her eyes.

The man wasn't hearing it. The bulge in his neck was bigger than the bulge in his pants at that time. Brandi put her hands over her head ashamed at being caught with her kids gawking at her mess. She looked at her husband knowing that he wasn't about to give in to Lexi's invitation no matter how much he may have been aroused by it. He suspected for a long time that something was going on but he could never put his finger on it working twelve hour shifts a day, six days a week.

"Lex, just go baby. Just go!" She yelled.

"Naw. Y'all ain't going nowhere. You wanna fuck? Then let's fuck!" The man yelled running to the closet for his shotgun.

Lexi didn't need any other cue but that one as she leapt off the bed grabbed her shoes and ran through the kids towards the front door. As she ran down the stairs of the project building she heard two loud booms coming from Brandi's floor. She stopped to cringe both times at the sounds hoping she was okay but it would be a cold day in hell before she went back to find out.

Chapter 19- Sweet Revenge

Nothing mattered anymore but vengeance. It seemed the thought was beginning to consume her. She yearned much more than that, however. They needed to feel the pain she would feel for the rest of her natural life. Diamond took a few hundred-dollar bills from the case then locked it and slid it under the bed. She looked at the mini bar and hit it hard drinking every little bottle of alcohol shots they stored in the room. It didn't hit her that she had mixed light and dark liquor until they were all gone, shaking her head at the sick feeling in the pit of her stomach. She passed out on the floor as the soothing sounds of Maxwell's Pretty Wings rung through her ears. She crawled to the nightstand her phone sat on and was shocked at what the display read.

"Now, what the fuck this bitch want?" She exclaimed tossing her phone to the side on the floor.

Diamond felt bubbling in her stomach and then a light headed dizzy feeling. She rose as did the chunks in her throat as she scurried to the toilet to blow in there. It felt good to release as she dry heaved what was left inside of her, collapsing on the side of the toilet still holding on.

She realized either the baby wasn't agreeing with the alcohol or her disease was kicking her ass in full force.

Lying next to the commode, smelling it's porcelain essence made her feel even sicker and lower than she had ever felt before. She looked down at the scratch on her leg left when the pastor ripped her panties trying to get inside her. She rubbed it bursting into a crying frenzy with huge raindrop like tears falling down her face. A small light bulb went off in her head prompting her to get up dizzily looking for her keys. It was time to talk.

She jumped in her rented ride and headed down the street like she was Speed Racer of the night. The windows were rolled down so she could stay awake letting the cool night wind slap her in the face mildly. She didn't have a thought in her head as she drove through red lights and ran stop signs. She dodged the few cars on the street whipping corners like there was no tomorrow. Whenever she spotted the police she straightened up getting her act together but once they were out of her sight she went right back to her speed demon tricks.

The house she pulled up in front of was all too familiar. It had only been a few weeks since she had been there but seeing it again was like reliving an old memory, you never forget. Diamond jumped out the car pushing the door drunkenly exiting. She slammed it hard not realizing then slowly made her way to the steps of the beautiful house. She whipped out her keys and opened the door feeling right at home. It was if she never left.

"Pastor." She yelled through the house causing an echo.

She got no response. It was eerily quiet and every corner was dark except for the little light that shined in the windows from the streetlights. She walked to the island in the kitchen tossing her keys on the counter, gazing through the darkness at what was once a beautiful home to her. She walked toward the knife block on the counter, sliding out the smallest one she could find and slipping it in her panties on top of her ass. Now all it was, was a pathway to hell. She walked to the fireplace where her mother's urn used to sit almost teary eyed at the fact that it was gone.

"What are you doing here, Diamond?" The pastor asked puffing away on his cigar.

Diamond noticed the red fire circle burning in the darkness near the couch. She couldn't see his face or even a silhouette of him but his voice was prominent. There were no words that she could speak to him. She headed over standing in front of him swaying slowly. He could not understand why she was over there after all the shit that happened between them. It was a trick and he knew it but he was too intoxicated to care. There were beer cans all over the living room floor where he was sitting and most had been there for days.

"Don't speak. I'm just gone give you what you want." Diamond said mounting him and kissing his neck slowly.

"Who said I wanted this?" He responded.

"I know you want it." She whispered nibbling on his ear.

"No. Get off me." The words flew out of the pastor's mouth but he did nothing to stop her actions.

Diamond continued her act. She moved down to his pants unbuckling them quickly and sifting his pants down roughly. He didn't fight her. The roles were reversed putting Diamond in control, which was something he hated dearly but his inebriation wouldn't allow him to refuse her advances. He threw his head back on the couch patiently awaiting her warm mouth on his growing piece. She slammed her mouth on his shaft swallowing as if it were a hot dog. She cuffed his balls in the palm of her hand massaging as he moaned uncontrollably.

He felt his temperature rise, choking on the cigar smoke. He rested his hand on the arm of the couch with it in his hand no longer able to smoke as her tongue made vibrating waves on his piece. The pastor was in deep with it and Diamond moved rapidly stroking his dick and slobbering simultaneously. Spit flew everywhere and his seat became moist as she allowed the drool to seep down in between his legs.

"I can't cum like this." The pastor exclaimed.

He staggered to his feet and Diamond never skipped a beat as she bobbed her head faster and faster sucking hard trying to make him cum in her mouth. She circled her tongue around the head of the shaft. It was surprising to her that she was enjoying the whole act.

It was the first time in a long time that she was willing to perform a sexual act without being forced into it. The pastor leaned his head back grabbing her head prompting her to go faster and faster. Diamond moaned heavily rubbing her clit so she could cum with him but the gyrating shaking motion coming from his legs indicated that he was already closer to it than she was.

"Yeah! Right there! Don't fucking move!" He moaned loudly.

Diamond felt his dick about to burst inside of her mouth. She prepared herself for the incoming as she choked and swallowed him sucking in all that she could of him. His legs locked down to the floor stiff as ever and his head cocked back pointed straight to the ceiling. He released into her mouth effortlessly pumping in her mouth and pushing her head towards him so she couldn't pull of so quick. Diamond had no intentions on coming up. She wanted all of him and wasn't going to stop until she had succeeded. He held her head still bursting all in her mouth to the very last drop. Diamond smiled at his attempt to choke her as she relaxed her throat allowing more room for him to push in further, then she chomped down as hard as she could.

"Arrrgggghhhhh!" The pastor screamed in agony.

He beat down on top of her forehead as hard as he could but it didn't seem to phase her one bit. She kept gnawing and chomping as if she was eating a robust steak dinner. Blood gushed from his groin and shot out like a fountain as she pulled and tugged for it to come off.

His punches gave way as his strength began to fade losing plasma rapidly. Diamond snatched her head off of him yanking hard pushing him back against the couch. Another good yank ripped the flesh entirely as she stood with her mouth full of the one thing he felt made him the ruler of his domain. She slipped it out of her mouth examining the broken piece of flesh curiously then licked her lips, smiling devilishly with satisfaction.

"Now you can call the police if you like but you should know that I'm going home to cook this up in my skillet with some good seasoning and I'm going to feast." Diamond said proudly.

The pastor sat on the couch applying as much pressure on the wound as possible unable to speak and barely able to breathe. He was in shock at the entire ordeal hoping she wouldn't let him sit there and bleed to death.

"You have one of two options. One, you can call the ambulance right away and they just may be able to save your ass or two bleed to death as I watch." Diamond spat looking down upon him. "If you choose option one but tell them what happened to you, you will die a slow and horrible death anyway. Choose wisely old man."

"Option one! Option one!" He screamed.

"Very good." She said clenching his dick tightly in her hand. "Oh and before I forget, you might want to give the paramedics a heads up that you might have AIDS."

Diamond walked out the door without a trace. His eyes bulged out ten times over as he tried to comprehend what she had just said to him. He lowered his head in utter disbelief wondering where his life went wrong and debating whether or not he should just lay there and bleed to death. In the back of his mind, he knew that he deserved every bit of bullshit that came his way nevertheless he wasn't apologetic for any of it. Diamond walked out of the door leaving him to stew in his own juices. She walked out of the house with his piece in tow and hopped into the car screeching off. Euphoria began to set in as the pastor reached in his pocket frantically pulling out his cell phone then dialing for help as he slowly passed out.

****

Diamond went to the Mobile gas station on 79th and Western snatching the bathroom key from the attendant's window without question. She went inside to clean herself, ridding herself of the blood prominent on her hands, clothes, and face. She took her tank top of and wrapped the pastor's piece in it then checked herself for any other traces of blood. She exited the station in just her purple lace bra and shorts, watching her surroundings closely keeping her senses open at all times.

The lot was empty as she threw the key on the counter then headed back to the car and drove off.

The only place Diamond could think to go was back to the condo the girls shared at one point. She fiddled through her keys before finding the right one and entered the place. It was dark appearing like no one was home but she learned her lesson the first time, not doubting it for a second. She headed straight for the kitchen tossing the shirt wrapped schlong on the counter as she looked through the cabinets for something to use on it. There was faint talking going on in one of the bedrooms but she couldn't make out if it was Lexi or Pandora's voice. Diamond began to panic, not wanting anyone to know what was in her tank top. She turned around facing the elongated sink then snatched the pastor's dick sticking it down into it. She stuffed and pushed but the son of a bitch wouldn't budge any further.

Diamond grew worried. She didn't really want to eat the damn thing but she did want it gone never to return to hurt anyone else under any circumstance. It was too dark for her to see her way into the drain to get it out. She cut the cold water on hoping it would soak the piece up a bit to be able to fit back through the hole.

She stuck her hand down in there but the sink didn't feel ordinary. As she flicked the switch directly above the faucet, a loud grinding noise erupted from the sink as little droplets of blood spewed up from the bottom. It startled her at first but then it all became clear what the noise was. Diamond cut the faucet off realizing it was gone without a trace and no one would be able to bring it back.

Chapter 20- Blood Ain't Too Thick

"Well, well, well. Look who came running back for some help." Pandora said as she slammed her phone down on the counter.

"I didn't come here to ask you for shit, P. I just needed to handle some business and now that I have I'm out." Diamond replied headed for the door.

"Leaving so soon?" Pandora asked stepping in her way. "You just got here. Sit. Talk. Let's catch up."

"Why?"

"I mean it's not everyday that I get to talk to my eldest sister and my twin at that." Pandora retorted as she pushed Diamond down on the sofa.

"I don't have time for bullshit, Pandora. I'd rather leave." Diamond spat, feeling as if her words weren't genuine.

"So, where have you been staying?" Pandora retorted quickly changing the subject.

"What do you care?"

"Alright listen you little bitch. I've tried to be nice long enough. Now here's how it's gonna go down. You're gonna sit here until these niggas come and whisk you away to hell so I can live happily ever after. Got it?" Pandora snapped pointing a finger in her face.

"Girl, you must truly be smoking something if you think I'm about to get caught up in your bullshit." Diamond spat rolling her eyes.

"No bullshit. They want you so they're gonna get you." Pandora turned away concealing her cell phone in her hand and reached into her pocket to pull out the figure's card.

"Move Pandora!" Diamond yelled.

"Or what?" Pandora smirked as she turned around with her phone to her ear.

Diamond slapped it out of her hand shattering it against the brick wall just barely missing the slim full-bodied mirror next to the bathroom. Pandora's eyes followed it and as it shattered so did her patience with Diamond. Rage ensued her as Pandora reached out to pound Diamond in the head with her fists. Diamond was not about to take an ass whopping lying down, grabbing her sister's hair and slamming her down to the ground like she was throwing down trash.

"You forgot I'm your older sister." Diamond bellowed triumphantly.

None of what she had to say was important, however. Pandora reached up pulling Diamond by her shorts trying to get her to the floor but she yanked away from her grip. She kicked her ankles hoping that she would fall flat on her face but Diamond held her ground keeping her feet planted to the floor.

She laughed as she began to kick her brutally. She kicked her in the forehead and the stomach not wanting to miss an inch of her ass.

"You are pathetic!" Diamond yelled hawking and releasing a huge glob of spit unto her eye.

Pandora screamed uncontrollably as if it were acid, grabbing her shirt to rub it away. She was so utterly disgusted that she began dry heaving onto the floor. Her phone was shattered on the floor in front of her and she didn't have a house phone. She needed Diamond's cell in order to make the call but getting it without a fight would prove to be a task in itself.

"Diamond, I'm sorry." Pandora confessed becoming teary eyed.

"Excuse me?"

"I'm sorry I failed you. We were supposed to stick together no matter what and I broke that bond on some selfish shit and for that, I'm sorry big sis." Pandora made every effort to sound sincere.

Diamond grew confused quickly. It was a sudden turn of events that she was not prepared for. Even though she hated who her sister had become and the way she went about doing things, that didn't take away from the fact that she loved her still. She helped Pandora up off the floor and flicked on the hall light anticipating finding authenticity in her eyes.

"Awe, lil sis. You didn't fail me. I failed you guys and myself. I should have been a better role model for y'all. That was my fuck up." Diamond spat.

Pandora headed for the living room as Diamond followed. The beautiful view of the city at night was breathtaking as the ladies stopped to bask in its splendor. Diamond still felt a bit uneasy about the situation but she didn't want to ruin the minute progress they were making towards renewing their relationship.

"Why are you in your bra, Di?" Pandora asked laughing.

"Oh…uh…girl it's a long story." Diamond joined in the laughter brushing the subject off.

"Well you can't be outside looking like that. I'll get you a shirt." Pandora said disappearing into the back room.

Diamond walked around the living admiring the great taste she had when she decorated it. Pandora did not want any of the color schemes she had picked out so she settled for what she wanted, which was everything in midnight blue.

The pool table in the raised part of the living room closest to the massive floor to ceiling windows was even midnight blue. Lexi never had an opinion on shit like that so the argument was between the twins and the whinier one won.

"You know, P, I hated the colors of the couches." Diamond made sure to laugh so she didn't come across as bitchy. "I mean we could've sparked a little purple or red in here, for real. What do you think?"

There was no response. She just assumed that she was so deep in the closet that she never heard her and it was good thing too. Pandora had a habit of taking things the wrong way and blowing them out of proportion. That wouldn't have done anything but sparked another argument and they would have been right back at square one again. Her thoughts danced around in her head about the night's events wondering if the pastor was still alive or not. No remorse filled her brain only questions. If he died, then she wouldn't be any better than Pandora. But revenge was revenge and it need to be served one way or the other.

"Damn sis. Did you have to make the shirt?" Diamond laughed as she bopped down the hall to Pandora's room.

The entire apartment was completely silent. There was not even a light on in the back where her room would be as Diamond neared. She pushed the door open and walked right in the room without any reservation and was immediately smacked in the front of her dome with a huge wooden bat. Her body fell like a ton of bricks to the floor. Pandora stood over her body looking down upon her like she had done her good deed.

"Ta-dow, bitch!" Pandora sat throwing the bat down, smiling and feeling good.

****

"Don't hang up." Lexi spat nervously breathing heavily on the phone.

"What do you want?"

"I can't stop thinking about you. We need to talk." Lexi said quietly.

"I don't think that's a good idea, Lexi."

"Oh yeah? Tell me you haven't been thinking about me and I will hang this phone up right now."

The phone was soundless. She listened closely waiting for the dreaded click that you hear before you actually realize you've been hung up on. The last thing he wanted to do was hang up on her and he knew it. They felt the same thing for each other despite the differences between them.

"Okay so I didn't hang up. So now what?" Kojack spat seemingly angry.

"So nothing. We need to meet up and talk face to face." Lexi spat smiling from ear to ear.

"Naw man, I'm afraid if I see you again, I'll engage in illegal activity, again."

"Awe. I'm flattered." She responded.

"That wasn't flattery. I can't get caught up in that shit with you girl. I mean, you bad and all but you jail bait. I can't get down." Kojack spat shaking and lowering his head as if she could see him.

"So you expect me to wait a whole year 'til I turn eighteen. Naw, that ain't gonna happen." Lexi spat.

"Naw, but…I'm confused like a motherfucka. I want you but I know it's wrong."

"Come meet me baby." Lexi retorted in a tiny seductive voice.

"No…no I can't do it girl." Kojack rebutted.

"You know, you don't strike me as a man who uses the word, can't." She spat quickly.

He couldn't help but to laugh. Kojack was stunned at the level of maturity Lexi displayed. She knew what she wanted and she went after it tenfold but knew how to remain subtle and still classy. It was beyond attractive; Kojack didn't know how to let go. Not to mention in a matter of speaking she was also his first. He caressed his chin thinking hard about what to do.

"You are something else. You know that?" He said smirking.

"So where you picking me up at?"

"Assertive, huh? Where are you?" He asked.

"On 55th, on the block." She replied hoping not to sound too anxious.

"Bet."

Lexi sauntered down the street towards Keisha house. She could see the entire block from her porch and was sure she wouldn't miss Kojack when he pulled up. The wooden stairs squeaked a bit as she crept up on them gradually. She didn't want to alert Keisha to her presence since she didn't feel like hearing her whine or helping her in the set.

****

Keisha paced back and forth through the set, watching the clock for quitting time. She was fed up with everyone. Her mother, Pandora and Lexi as far as she was concerned could kiss her where the sun didn't shine. Up walked a dark skinned, rather muscular man with jeans and a navy blue tank top. He didn't resemble any of the other cluckers that normally came for some work so she knew he couldn't have been there for that. She sucked her stomach in as tight as she could and sauntered over to the man halting him at the garage opening.

"Can I help you?" She smiled serving her large girls up in his face.

"Yeah, you can give me one of those thangs. You know what I'm saying?" He replied flirting back.

"Thangs? Now what would you want with that mess?" Keisha spat looking down at his fresh pair of Jordan's.

"That's my business. Isn't it?" The man replied trying to skate around her to get inside the garage.

Keisha eagerly walked in front of him blocking his view. She wasn't interested in selling him any bags, only herself. But he was more focused on the set. He bumped up against her protruding belly prompting her to release it, as it flopped down in front of her. It was a relief to her as she gasped for air, unable to hold it anymore. The man laughed as he looked down at it poking it like she was a Teletubby, then caressed his six-pack abs dancing them around in her face. Keisha swooned at the sight, drooling over and begging to lick them.

"What did you say you wanted again?" She salivated.

"Gimme two of them thangs, girl." He said licking his lips.

Keisha reached in her jogging pants pocket and pulled out two small Baggies. She exchanged the merchandise from his hand and took the money from his under hand. Her finger sensually seduced the palm of his hand as she removed it, sliding her hand on her hip.

"So, is there anything else I can do for you?" Keisha asked licking her lips and sizing him up.

The man looked around the dark garage then turned his attention back on the voluptuous woman in front of him. What Keisha did not know was that, he had just gotten out of jail only a few weeks before and he was in heat like a dog who had just hit puberty.

He hadn't had any from a woman in years so the fact that she was a big girl wasn't a problem for him. He reached up, pulling the old flimsy garage door down leaving it open a little at the bottom but it was still completely dark inside. Keisha heard rattling figuring he was undressing for her and turned needing to find the light fast. She leaned against the wall waiting for him to feel his way through the darkness and come to receive her. She waited and waited then listened and heard nothing but silence. Pissed off, Keisha made her way feeling the walls tracking to the light fixture on the wall next to the house door and flicked the switch.

GASP!

Chapter 21- Trust Me

"Mmm. Mmm."

Diamond grumbled reaching for her head but was halted by the rope that bounded her hands and feet behind her back. She was no stranger to concussions by now with her blurry vision and blood that oozed from her hair. Nonetheless, she was determined to pull it together to get the fuck out of there. She wiggled her hands and feet trying to get them loose but it was no use. The rope was extremely tight, almost cutting off the circulation in her wrists. Her vision began to come to as she squinted her eyes attempting to focus.

"Welcome back." Pandora said circling her sister.

"What the fuck are you doing, Pandora?" Diamond snapped.

"Oh it's quite simple. You are going down for Sun's murder and stealing his shit."

"What?"

"Yeah, they want Diamond so they're gonna get Diamond." Pandora laughed bringing her suitcases out of the room placing them next to the door. "So when they get here, you'll be dead and I'll be in the

Bahamas somewhere sipping a Mai Tai under the Island sun."

Laughter filled Diamond's face. Dying in any form was the biggest joke of all to her. It didn't bother her one bit to die anymore, especially not since after the news of her condition. She was actually grateful that someone was about to put her out of her misery and that she didn't have to wait for the disease to do it for her. Diamond wiggled some more than began laughing hysterically again.

"You think I'm worried about someone killing me? Poor Pandora. You're even more fucked up then I originally thought." Diamond continued to laugh.

"It doesn't matter 'cause you'll be dead. One less bitch I gotta worry about." Pandora smirked.

"Shit, you got that now, trick. 'Cause don't think for one second you ain't dead to me."

"You'd just better hope they call Lex to identify the body 'cause the city can have your ass for all I care, Di—."

"GREAT! A real fucking burial!" Diamond retorted shaking her head at her sister's ignorance.

Pandora had had enough of the bullshit between them. She began picturing that bitch dead in the middle of some brutal and bloody scene and instantly became so happy that a malevolent smile appeared on her face. Her thoughts fueled her ambition to keep the plan going but the icing on the cake would have been Diamond begging like a peasant for her life. It angered her than even though her life hung in the balance she was still the same old smart aleck bitch.

"Boy I can't wait til you're dead. Then I never again have to utter the words, I'm a twin." Pandora said in a wicked manner.

"As if being you is so damn great. But you've always wanted to be me haven't you? You're nothing but a fucked up clone of me. The egg split by mistake you dumb ass." Diamond said spitting far but missing Pandora terribly.

"Ha! You can't do anything right. Can you?" Pandora laughed.

"Oh you'll be amazed at what I can do." Diamond retorted.

Pandora reached down digging through Diamond's pockets searching for her cell phone, pulling it out of her back pocket. Diamond leaned in to bite her on the cheek but failed miserably. Pandora spat at her face coming within inches of her mouth but missed as it splatted on the side of the chair. She walked towards her shattered phone retrieving the business card and began dialing the number.

"Yeah, this is Diamond. I got your shit." Pandora spat as she gave the man the address to their apartment.

"Do you have any idea what kind of danger you've put Lex in?" Diamond spat heatedly.

"Lex? Who gives a shit about that ho?" Pandora laughed as she threw Diamond's phone down to the floor. "Later sis oh and uh, a word of advice. Close your eyes. It won't hurt as much."

Pandora picked up her freshly packed bags and skirted out the door frantically without a trace. Diamond looked down at her phone, which sat a few feet away from her. She knew she had to reach it if she wanted to survive but that would prove difficult with her hands and feet bound to the metal chair. Tears filled her eyes but never fell as she thought about giving up and letting whatever happened to her happened. *I'm fucked anyway.* She thought.

****

The phone kept ringing over and over again before going to the voicemail. Lexi didn't have any other number on Keisha as she repeatedly dialed her number desperate to get in contact with her. She didn't want to wake her mother up especially in her fragile state but she was nearing Keisha's house and needed a place to post up and wait for Kojack. She reached the porch, looking all around the windows for one with a spec of light shining through one of them but came up short. She stood out on the porch looking up and down the street praying he pulled up soon. Somebody catching her in the hood with him and reporting it back to Pandora was all she needed at this point in time.

"Damn. It took you long enough." Lexi said to herself as she crept off of Keisha's porch and up to Kojack's car.

He exited the car to open her car door, perplexed since no man or woman for that matter had ever done that for her before. She politely waited for him to open it as she got in and allowed him to close the door behind her.

Fancy. She thought with a surprised look on her face. He entered and drove off peeping her shock at his gentleman like behavior.

"So where we going?" He asked checking his nicely lined goatee in the rearview mirror.

"Where do you wanna go?" She replied seductively rubbing the nape of his neck with her fingertips.

Kojack was like putty in her hands, as his neck grew stiff as well as his Johnson. He felt like if he moved she would take that as a hint to stop and he couldn't have that happen especially not when it felt so damn good. He hopped on the expressway headed for the one place he was very sure they would be alone with no interruptions. Lexi moved her hands down to his zipper undoing it swiftly. She gazed at him noticing his smile widen as she released his limp schlong from his drawers and brought it up for some air.

"Girl, you know I'm driving right?" He said preparing himself for what was about to happen.

Lexi didn't mutter a word. She released herself from her seatbelt then propped up on all fours throwing her juicy ass against the window. Kojack didn't have tinted windows on his front two windows so her ass was plastered against the glass for all to see.

He kept his eyes on the road as best he could trying not to crash but her ass kept calling him to look at it. She twerked it for him then began bouncing one cheek at a time as he reached his strong-arm around to give her ass a loving smack. Lexi was wild in ways that other women he had dealt with never was. But the only problem was that she wasn't a woman, yet. He couldn't help but think about that aspect because if anyone ever found out about their love affair he would surely end up in jail.

She grabbed his dick stroking it lustily and giving the head sweet wet kisses to tease him. Kojack's legs began to sway with anticipation wanting the action to start already. He knew what he was in store for and he couldn't wait any longer for her to dig in. Lexi leaned her head over further placing his dick in her mouth and sucking soft yet hard at the same time. He tried not to lean his head back in enjoyment, trying to remain focused on the road, but the good head he was receiving distracted his good judgment. The car began to sway from side to side making Lexi nervous.

"Don't crash baby." She spat sweetly.

"Oh, I'm not. You just keep doing what you doing. I got this." He replied giving her head a soft nudge.

That was her cue to go to work on his ass. She spat on his piece letting slob trail from her mouth to his shaft raising her head high enough to show the display then going back down fast and hard sucking with every motion. Kojack tried to resist the urge to moan but it flowed out of his mouth like water from a faucet. His moans became louder and louder making him feel inferior in a way wondering how she was doing those circular tricks with her tongue that caused him to scream like that.

He grabbed every bit of strength he could muster and focused in hard on the road, rushing to their destination. He knew that she would never let up on him long enough to get there and truth be told he wasn't in the mood to stop her. Her mouth felt like fresh Gain smelling cotton drawers out of the dryer, damn good.

"Do you like that, daddy?" She asked rising up for only a split second.

"Hell, yeah!" Kojack exclaimed feeling himself about to burst.

Not yet. Not yet. He thought as he swerved off the road towards their exit. The closer he got to their spot the closer she came to making him burst in her mouth. Lexi liked swallowing cum. It was like nourishment to her when she didn't get it from anywhere else and she wanted to swallow his badly. Her pussy throbbed tremendously knowing his time was near. As she moaned with a mouth full of meat, Kojack bellowed behind her as he slowed the car down coming to a stop. He was there and she knew it. She began sucking harder and harder then flickering her tongue on his head bobbing faster on his piece.

"Ooo, shit!" Kojack screamed in a high-pitched voice.

"Mmmm!" Lexi retorted never skipping a beat.

Kojack held on to the steering wheel for dear life as she sucked him high and dry. She continued to bob even though she had already taken in all he had to give.

His body shifted searching for a position where he could stand the high intensity of oral pleasure he was receiving. Lexi finally released him from her oral fixation wishing she hadn't since she still wasn't satisfied. She sat back in her seat with the ugliest frown upon her face.

"Man, I don't know how you do it but damn girl!" Kojack said.

"Thanks." She replied wiping the drool from her lips.

"Well what's wrong?" He asked perplexed.

Lexi reached into her pocket fumbling through then pulled out a Yomper popping it in her mouth undetected. She sat back letting the affects of the drug flow through her veins and soothe her organs. Her eyes rolled to the back of her head, partially fulfilled as she ran her fingers through her hair feeling extra sensitive to every touch. She could feel her blood run coldly through her veins but with every touch Kojack delivered, she melted.

"I'm still not happy." Lexi responded.

"Oh yeah." Kojack spat moving his hand down in between her legs.

She waited to see what he was diving at before she became excited. He was fingering around outside of her pants figuring that would make her insanely moist but it didn't. Lexi was already moist she needed to bust to relieve her stress. She sighed loudly hoping she would not have to instruct him to give her what she needed. She hated that. Kojack reached around unbuttoning her pants and scooting them down to her ankles.

Lexi kicked them off with haste allowing her red panties to follow then positioned her legs across the steering wheel and the back of his seat. Kojack brushed her pretty nicely shaved brown pussy with the back of his hand loving the way her soft skin felt against his. He looked at the discerning look on her face and realized he wasn't doing his job right.

He reached under her pulling her ass cheeks closer to him then faced his body toward her stretching his torso to reach her small clit. The anticipation busted inside of her much like she wanted her cum to in his mouth. Lexi pulled the lips of her pussy open wide enough for him to attack her clit with no problem. He dove in sucking on her pretty little pleasure nub like it was a straw. He slurped and licked making loud noises, torturing her button with his tongue as if he wanted her to scream. Lexi felt her legs tremble but she remained calm wanting to indulge in all of his erotic performance. Kojack slipped his tongue into her slit fucking her like it was his rock hard dick going in and out then he took his index and middle finger sticking them both in as far as he could. His reach excited her more as she felt her climax rise even more.

Kojack hummed lightly sending vibrations through her body titillating her soul. Lexi thought she was in heaven from the perfect feeling shooting through her right then. She gripped the back of his head tightly not wanting to let go even though he was signaling for air.

Her mind wasn't focused on him any longer, it was her turn to get off and she was not about to let up until she did. The feeling was just like the last time and even though it felt like nothing more than pure unadulterated sex, it was the grandest either of them had ever experienced.

"I love it when you eat it."

Lexi could feel her climax reach its boiling point and there was no way for her to compose herself. She moaned irrepressibly making high pitched screeching noises as she struggled to breathe. Her grip tightened on his head so he didn't move from the good spot and throw the whole mood off. She fucked his mouth back as he moved his tongue rapidly giving her clit a well-deserved lashing. Lexi grabbed her nipples flicking them fast to aid in her pleasure as she released significantly into his awaiting mouth. Kojack sucked all that she had given him with no problem as she rolled her hips around enjoying every minute of it. She was more than ready for her dick now as he mounted her without question ready to give it to her deep.

CRASH!

Chapter 22- Just Got Real

Keisha jumped back staring into the eyes of four dudes standing next to the man she thought she was about to fuck. She wanted to reach for her piece but she knew them niggas wouldn't come up in there deep and not be strapped. It was in her best interest to play in cool at first to feel those niggas out but her first mind told her to give them whatever the hell they wanted because her life wasn't worth a few measly dollars from Pandora's stingy ass.

"What y'all niggas want?" She spat rocking back and forth and slapping her hands together.

"I think you know what we what. Where did you get this shit? Before you answer that, you should know that the streets been talking. So we know who you are already." The man said winking his eye at her with a smirk.

"I saw a man about a dog. What of it?" Keisha spat sarcastically.

The men were not amused by her bullshit comment. They neared her watching as she stepped further away from them, backing into the garage wall.

"My patience is wearing thin. So where did you get this shit?" The man asked again pointing a shiny silver Glock in her direction.

"I don't know where it came from. Somebody gave it to me alright." She exclaimed putting her hands up.

"Who?" The men seem to ask simultaneously.

Keisha wanted to hesitate but she knew they would surely kill her if she did. These men apparently meant business and she wasn't about to die over some shit she never wanted to be apart of in the first place. She looked down at the ground then back up into their eyes opening her mouth to tell them just what they wanted to hear.

"It was Pandora Burden. She used to stay in Evergreen. That's all I know." Keisha said feeling a sense of relief to finally get that off her chest to someone.

"Keisha? What's going on in there?" Ms. Rita said pushing the house door to the garage open.

"Nothing mama. Go back to bed." Keisha yelled not wanting her mother to die of grief from the sight of the men.

The men stood there as still as bats when they sleep not wanting to make any sudden moves when grandma walked through the door. They prepared themselves to leave searching around the garage for traces of the rest of the merchandise. Keisha glanced over to the old wooden desk in the corner hoping they didn't go over there and find the rest of the stash.

"Got it boss." One of the men exclaimed as he threw the uncut brick to the main man.

"It's not mine." Keisha said shaking her head, silently asking herself why she got involved with this bullshit in the first place.

Ms. Rita heard loud talking coupled with a bunch of commotion going on in the back of the house. It was impossible to miss since her window was right in the backyard and with the garage windows raised you could hear virtually everything that was going on. She knew some shit wasn't right as she rose from the bed preparing her self for the worst. From the sound of it, it sounded like they were being robbed. Ms. Rita grabbed the phone and dialed Pandora but as usual there was no answer. She left a message.

"Bitch you need to get over here asap! Somebody is stickin' us up!"

Once she hung up that called she had a bad feeling. She grabbed her bitch out from under the bed and cocked her like it was nothing. Her strength was minimal but that wasn't going to stop her from saving the only person she ever loved. Before she walked out the door, though, she made yet another call.

"911 Emergency."

"Yes, I need the ambulance and the police to 805 W. 55th. It's urgent! Come quick! There are multiple gunshots!" Ms. Rita exclaimed as she hung up the phone.

She knew that even in the hood an abrupt hang up gets them fools there faster every time. Her footsteps were small yet swift as she muscled all of her energy for an all out brawl with whomever was back there fucking with her child.

As she neared the garage door the voices became louder and more prevalent as if they were torturing Keisha to tell them information. She took the biggest gulp she had ever taken before in her life then looked up to the sky. *Honey, I'm coming home.* She thought.

"Keisha, what the fuck is going on in here?" Ms. Rita said busting in the door startling all the young men. "Oh hell naw!"

Ms. Rita pulled her long black nine-millimeter from behind her back barely able to hold it straight and began blasting those dudes in their faces. She didn't have much strength in her right arm but she went in guns blazing, no holds bar on them niggas without a care, pushing Keisha to the ground. She blasted one right after another feeling like she had the upper hand on their asses but she wasn't about to do a victory dance until all of them were spread eagle on the ground and they were all leaking.

"Ahh!" Ms. Rita roared, continuing to bust at those fools.

"Y'all done fucked up now!" Keisha yelled pulling out her piece, wailing back at those niggas.

The gunfire went on for a few minutes striking down two of the men there and throwing a couple in Ms. Rita. Keisha got up off the floor busting her chop at the main nigga not wanting him to get away especially since he played her in the beginning. She fire twice at him and he fired once hitting her dead in between the eyes and grazing her left ear. She hit the floor deader than a doorknob.

Ms. Rita was curdling on her own blood, fidgeting her feet and hands seemingly trying to escape the catastrophe she had created but not getting anywhere with her scooting. Only two men remained as the others lay on the floor with bullets to the brain, not breathing.

"We just got that call man. We gotta ride." The remaining man spat.

"Ay yo, check that bitch's pockets for dough." Shug said as he walked over staring down at Ms. Rita puffing for air. "And grab that work out of there and mount up."

Shug had stepped away then gawked back as they raised the garage door ready to leave. He looked down at his buddies shaking his head at them. There was no remorse cause they were killed by two bitches who weren't shit in his eyes. His buddy pulled the truck around signaling out the window for him to bring his ass before anybody saw them. Shug nodded his head toward him them looked back to see if Ms. Rita had gone yet. She had taken a lickin' and kept on tickin' determined to be ruthless until her last breath. Shug plowed two to her dome, easy, and then ran off to the truck.

    ****

Diamond wobbled the chair left and right trying to reach deep down in her drawers for the sharp object sticking her in the ass. She had originally put it there for use as revenge on the pastor but she had sought a much more powerful and tastier one then just slicing his throat.

Her fingertips touched the top of the blade's handle while she scooted back and forth trying to push it upward and out. She strained and flinched as the blade poked her numerous times. The handle slipped back down in her panties. Damn. She thought. She tried again to fish the knife out of her pants, struggling and cutting herself along the way. It was out.

The phone began to ring, startling her like crazy. Diamond frenziedly positioned the knife strategically in her hand trying to cut the cord she was bound with. Even though the rope was impossible to escape by her own force it was rather thin and cut easily. She freed her hands first then her feet dropping the knife and removing the rope quickly as she grabbed her phone and jetted for the door. At the door she listened to see if she could hear anyone in the hallway. Silence was golden to her as she opened the door prepared to run down to the end of the hall to the elevator. She opened the door running smack dab into a large broad chest.

"Leaving so soon." The man said entering the apartment.

He backed Diamond up forcing her back into the apartment shutting the door behind him. She looked around to see if anyone was behind him but oddly he was alone. The fact that Pandora had sent one lonely nigga over there to kill her was laughable. Diamond could drop him like a bad habit with no problem. Her confidence boosted an extra inch. She glanced over at the knife on the floor then back at the man not wanting to alarm him of her plan.

"Where's the shit, Diamond?" He spat flexing his muscles.

"Okay, check it. I'm Diamond but I'm not who you think I am. I know that sounds fucked up but it's real shit."

"What the fuck does that have to do with my man's shit?" The man said as his cell phone buzzed in his pocket.

He wanted to ignore it but it began to buzz abundantly. His large hand removed it from his back pocket answering it.

"Yeah."

"Yo. We got the merch." Shug said.

"One." The man replied hanging up the phone. "So we got our shit. I guess this is goodbye."

"WAIT! You got the wrong bitch. Please!" Diamond said putting her hands up. "I know who killed Sun!"

Diamond closed her eyes preparing for the bullet to crack through her skull. All that could be heard in the room was dead silence. So dead, in fact, that she believed she was just that. She squinted one eye open, hawking around the room peeping to see what he was doing. The man dropped the weapon to his side.

"I'm listening." He spat.

"Okay. This may be hard for you to believe but...I have a twin. Her name is Pandora and she is this one who killed him." Diamond spat quickly.

The man looked at her side eyed before raising his gun back up to her face. "Is this some kind of joke?"

"NO! Please! It's no joke. I have a twin a she is the bitch behind all of this. She just left here not too long ago and she's trying to frame me so she can get off scott free with her boyfriend." Diamond caught her breath from nervousness. "In fact I think I know where she's headed."

He didn't know if he should believe anything she was saying but he was intrigued to know if she was telling the truth about having a twin. It really didn't matter to him either way. They both had to die in his eyes; he didn't have time for snitches or setups. The man scratched his head wondering what he should do knowing Tino wouldn't want any stray enemies out there. He slapped his gun behind his back and grabbed Diamond by the arm escorting her to the door.

"If you lying, you're fucking dead on the spot." He spat furiously.

He had already had it in the back of his mind to kill them both on the spot anyway but he remained cool so he could at least get to the other one, killing two birds with one stone. Diamond had a feeling she was dead on the spot one way or the other. She had to think fast because if she got in the car with him she was surely dead. She yanked her arm back as quickly as possible but tried to remain friendly to keep him cool, calm, and collected.

"Wait. If she sees you she'll know something is up and try to run. The only way to get her is to follow behind my car so she doesn't see you. Then you can sneak up on her and do what you need to do as far as I'm concerned." Diamond said.

"Don't try anything stupid or that's your ass." The man watched as she walked to her vehicle parked out front and jumped in his.

He never took his eye off of her; he knew if he lost her it would be his ass on the line. Diamond pulled out slowly keeping a side eye on him through the rear view mirror. She pulled out her cell phone dialing sluggishly on the keypad as not to alarm her voyeur of her actions.

"Yeah, I got some information that you might be interested in." Diamond spat as she revealed her destination. "Meet me there in thirty minutes and you'll have your man."

Diamond smiled to herself checking her mirror making sure he was still back there. She fixed her hair glancing slightly back and forth in the mirror keeping the car straight on the road at the same time. It needed to be on point for the gathering they were on their way to. She couldn't let her old flame and her ex-sister see her looking a hot mess. The only thing she was missing was dark red lipstick to complete her devilish look. *That bitch has got another thing coming if she thinks I'm going quietly into the night.* Diamond thought.

Chapter 23- Busted

"Freeze motherfucker and put your hands in the air!" The male cop yelled pointing his pistol right for his targets head.

Shug was half way in the car before he was startled by the onset of a plethora of cops surrounding him. The fight in him erupted not wanting to go down without one. The gun in his hands was still warm from the shots he had just blazed into Keisha and her mother but he knew it would be on fire if he shot at those huff ass cops. They kept yelling violent obscenities attempting to get the men to lay down and lower their weapons.

"Man Shug, I ain't know we was gon' be on some Set It Off shit, g. I mean we done kid." Shug's partner, Flex said with tears forming in his eyes.

"You a fucking bitch dude. Just get in the damn car so we can peel out." Shug exclaimed.

Flex gave him the side eye then took a glance over at all of the guns pointing to their heads. He wasn't prepared to die that way, not for Shug or anybody.

The other guys scooted down in the back seats struggling not to be seen and pushing the money and dope under them.

A tired Flex gave Shug a solemn look then shook his head in disagreement placing his hands in the air to surrender. The facial expression on Shug's face went from angry to sinister in a matter of seconds as he reluctantly put his hands in the air as well.

"Step away from the vehicle, drop down to your knees and put your hands on your head!" The cop's voice echoed through the bullhorn harshly.

"Ay motherfucka. This ain't over by a long shot. You heard me?" Shug recited before Flex vanished from sight onto the ground.

"Down on the fucking ground. NOW!" One of the cop's screamed.

The man simply cocked his attention towards the approaching cops unaffected by his threat and waited to be hand cuffed. He knew eventually he would have to deal with Shug in jail but he didn't care about that either. He had seen everything in this world accept Christ and whether it be by Shug's hand or the hand of the disease eating away at his immune system he knew he would see him soon. Shug watched as the cops carried him away to the paddy wagon and prayed like hell they put him in the same truck so he could have his last few words with him.

The cops checked out the crime scene beginning with the truck Shug and Flex were standing in front of.

They opened it up completely and found the other two dudes cowering like cowards in the back seat. One of the cops laughed at their pitiful faces not the least bit phased by their attempt to look innocent. He signaled for his partner to aid him in securing the newfound suspects. With Shug cuffed still on the ground, they removed his counterparts from the truck and placed them right next to him.

"Looky here Sarg. We rounded up a few more." One of the cops yelled happily.

The men looked over at Shug ready to kick his ass if it weren't for their hands being restrained. They each cringed with hatred but was distracted by the sound of the cops raising the garage door. It was like a scene out of a Charles Dickens horror novel. The brain matter splattered all over the place made everyone sick to their stomachs. It was all they could do not to throw up on the crime scene. The Sergeant even had a hard time looking in the garage and he was a twenty-five year veteran.

"What the hell is that?" The Sergeant questioned.

"I believe that's the brain of the younger female victim. It appears to be oozing out of her head." One of the cops answered.

"Why the fuck did you shoot these women? This one has a medical night gown on." He jolted back at the suspects. "Boy, you son of a bitches gon' fry for this one. I'll tell you what."

The Sergeant backed out of the scene allowing for the others to do their jobs and clean up the mess. He wasn't prepared for that display but choked it up as usual so he could make it through the rest of the day without dwelling on it. The first thing that came to his mind was to kick all of the men in their genitals a few times but it wouldn't have made a difference, it wouldn't have given those women their lives back. The second thought he had was to spit on them but he didn't want to put a slew of decorated cops through the humiliation of getting on the stand to lie for him so he simply just walked away.

"Sergeant Brian Sutters." The Sergeant said answering his cell phone.

"Are you still coming?"

"I said I'd be there. I'm kind of in the middle of something right now." He responded angrily.

"Well you'd better hurry up cause I'm almost there."

The party on the other line hung up on him. He looked at the phone angrily as if it were the person then threw it back in his pocket. He took one last look at the scene then decided to head out to see what was so urgent that he needed to meet now. The cops were just about done taking pictures and the detectives out there were gathering up all of the evidence they needed before the coroner's office scraped what was left of Ms. Rita and Keisha's bodies up off the garage floor.

"I want these scum bags in the truck and behind me now. I want to book these assholes myself."

Sutters recited as he headed for his unmarked squad car.

"Yes sir." One of the cops assured him as he began loading the suspect into the paddy wagon.

Inside of the wagon, the men all looked at each other but never spoke a word. They were all waiting for the right time to speak so they didn't alert the cops to their discussion. A few minutes passed before they heard the sounds of the front doors slamming and the truck starting. They were finally hitting the road, anxious to use that noise as their diversion to talk. Shug stared directly at Flex waiting to get his attention but when he never looked his way he refused to wait any longer.

"So you that kind of nigga, huh?" Shug said sucking his teeth as if there was meat in them.

"Man, I ain't got time for your shit. We caught. Get over it." Flex responded.

"Get over it huh? That's big talk from a lame ass nigga who's gon' get his ass whooped when we get in lockup." Shug threatened.

Flex shook his head carelessly and smiled while sucking his teeth at the same time. "Do you honestly think I give a fuck about you trying to whoop my ass? The only thing I gave a fuck about was you fucking me in it."

"What? Man ain't nobody on that gay shit with you, man. You betta calm that gay shit down, for real." Shug began to sweat bullets from his forehead.

He couldn't believe this nigga had outted him like that even after their pact of secrecy. The threats he was sending out were only meant to scare him not to testify against him during trial but Flex was kicking out the big guns and he wasn't done yet. With the smirk oddly placed on his face, he decided it was time to let the cat out of the bag.

"Yeah motherfucka, you're gay. You're just as fucking gay as I am and the fact that you think it's cute to deny it makes you all the more gay." Flex chuckled.

His words only angered Shug even more than he already was. "Shut the fuck up!"

"No! I will not shut the fuck up boo boo dick and you know something else? Tino is way better fuck than you baby. Yeah. He's my bitch for life you can't touch that." Flex began laughing so hard that his stomach began to ache. "But that's still not the home stretch. He has had AIDS for the longest time and so have I. Boom!"

Everyone in the back of the wagon stared at Flex then back at Shug. They were waiting for the explosion to happen. Flex had a menacing looking smile on his face coupled with heavily squinted eyes like he was teasing him. If it weren't for his shackles being cuffed to the seat he would've gotten up a long time ago and launched at his ass.

"Listen I ain't got time to be listening to this shit. You lie so fucking much it's pathetic, yo. So fuck what you talkin' 'bout you can kiss my ass." Shug tried to remain calm but he couldn't deny that it felt like that of ticks eating away at his insides.

"Oh but you will listen. Because in a few months when the prison tests you and they figure out what you have who will be kissing who's ass, sugar?"

Flex blew a kiss then stuck his tongue out at him flicking it, working it, and rolling it like the ocean current. By now, the other men had begun to look away uninterested in anymore of the conversation. It was shocking and interesting in the beginning but the topic was not one that they were prepared to tolerate listening to. Shug's face resembled that of a raging bull, wanting to run Flex right on over.

"Why wouldn't you have told me this shit before?" Shug asked shortly.

"Oh. Now that wouldn't have been much fun, huh? We've been fucking around for a whole year so whatever I got you got baby." Flex laughed winking his eye playfully. "And would you have even cared? Naw boo. All you cared about was fucking me so you could feel like you had one up on Tino, right?"

"It's on bitch. It's on."

"Karma is a bitch. You really should reevaluate yourself as a person before you treat people like shit. I'm not scared of you and as a matter of fact, I bet those women back there that tried to blow your head off weren't scared either." Flex shook his head looking out of the caged window. "They should've blasted your weak ass."

"You betta watch your damn mouth. Shit it's because of you I'm even in this mess." Shug replied.

"No. You should probably watch your mouth. You don't want any of those prison dudes to mistake your ass whole for a shitting hole. 'Cause I will tell them you like the boys and have for very long time." Flex laughed.

The truck came to a halt. Shug stretched his body as far as he could to look out of the caged window to where they were and what was gong on. There were so many trees outside they thought they were about to get murdered by some cops in broad daylight. The looked to the other side of the truck then realized they hadn't obviously reached their destination yet. Thumbing and banging on the side of the truck forced them to be even nosier than they already were. They just wanted to be aware of their surroundings so they didn't miss their chance to get away if they could. The cops were on the side of the truck filling it up with gas.

There were so many people in the gas station and not one of those people could help them even if they wanted too. After a few doughnuts and cups of coffee the cops jumped their out of shape asses back into the truck and pulled off. All Shug could think about was how long it was going to take them to drive that big ass truck to the They were done for and it was time to face the music but Shug wasn't ready too. He couldn't wait to get to the jailhouse so he could call his well paid lawyer and get out. He could've posted bail for Flex too but since he played him with bitch moves he was going to let him fester in there until his court day. *For that nigga's sake he better be lying about that shit, straight up.* Shug thought.

Chapter 24- You're Done

Pandora hopped out of the car not even thinking to survey the damage she had just caused to her rental. She walked up to the car to see what bitch this nigga had in his car. Her fists pounded like rolling thunder on the trunk then the windows as she walked to the side of the car peeking inside. The windows were slightly fogged by the activity inside but it was still visible enough to see bodies meshing together. They looked so loving, so passionate, and it churned in her mind like butter fucking with her mental and destroying her heart.

"Come out of there you son of a bitch! This how you gon' do me?" Pandora spat watching Kojack pull his pants up back around his waist.

He pulled his .45 out from under his seat then exited the car ready to blow her head off. Kojack walked up to her posted nose to nose with his lips and eyes curled over angrily. The stench of Lexi's pussy eroded from his breath as he huffed and puffed in her face. His intimidation was enough to stop a pit bull but she stood her ground unafraid of his testosterone show.

"Nigga you could miss me with that shit. Who the fuck you got up in there?" Pandora snapped.

"Bitch is you crazy? You fucked up my shit!" Kojack retorted waving his gun around wildly.

"Who is she, Kojack? Huh? Who the fuck is she?" Pandora yelled fighting to get past him to get to the car.

Lexi dressed slowly then exited the car not amused by Pandora's little act. She massaged her neck briefly before slamming the door and joining Kojack in the altercation. She muffed the shit out of Pandora before he broke them up holding his arms out to keep them apart.

"I should slap the dog shit out of you!" Lexi spat moving as slick as a ninja trying to get through Kojack to get to her.

"So what bitch! You always trying to get what I got. You just a fucking leach!" Pandora snapped back.

"Pandora, we through man! We been done. Get that shit through your fucking head." Kojack snapped grabbing Lexi by her waist pulling her back lovingly.

"So now you with this bitch?" Pandora said reaching over him to slap Lexi.

Lexi reached grabbing a fist full of Pandora's hair pulling her head down and beating her in the face. She was elated at finally having the upper hand, elated to finally let her know who was boss. She beat her on top of her head keeping her grip nice and tight hoping to yank a huge chunk of hair out of her head. Kojack hawked at Lexi something evil like.

"Babe, let her punk ass go. You got her babe, now just let her weak ass go." Lexi focused in on his charismatic persona and felt compelled to listen to him.

She released Pandora who jerked back fixing her hair and checking to see if she had many bruises and scratches. Pandora walked back to the car looking for something she could use to inflict pain upon the both of them simultaneously. She rummaged through the trunk finding a small crowbar under the spare tire gripping it tightly in her hands.

"Yippie ka-ye, motherfucka!" Pandora screamed as she climbed on top of Kojack's car smashing out the windows one by one.

He didn't even care about that shit anymore. She was the one looking like the fool. He had want he wanted, Lexi. They shook their heads at her stupidity then he placed his finger gently on Lexi's chin moving her lips up to his as he kissed her passionately revealing tongue to prove it was intimate. Pandora completely lost her mind, jumping off the car with the crowbar in the air headed towards them, screaming in disbelief. Kojack raised his gun back up to her face allowing her to stare down its long dark barrel.

"Don't trip. You done." He said speaking through his teeth.

"She's a fucking child, Kojack. That makes you a child molester." Pandora spat.

"I'll be seventeen soon and he ain't even thinking about that. This pussy got him gone bitch. Something you could never do." Lexi said curling her lips.

"Oh yeah? You wasn't complaining about my pussy when you was all up in it." Pandora wailed back.

"Who said it was good? It might have tasted good but bitch you ain't shit but dead weight. I got your man and he craves the shit out of this. Deal with that." Lexi retorted.

Pandora boiled over. She didn't know what to do looking back at Kojack wondering if there were any signs of love still left inside of him for her. The magic they shared seemed to have dissipated in no time. Her heart plummeted to the bottom of her feet seeing him hold her affectionately the way he was. She wanted to reach out and snatch that bitch by the throat and toss her in Lake Michigan never to be see or heard from again. The one sister she figured would never do her dirty no matter what she did to her turned out to be the one to stab her in the back times ten. She turned her attention to him hoping to get through to him.

"Kojack, what happened to us baby? We had so much more than just fucking. We had it all and now you gonna throw us away for this?" Pandora spat pointing to her sister, frowning.

Kojack didn't bat an eye at her interrogations even with her conjuring up some tears for a sympathy display. Her shoulders became weak as she held her arms up trying to get him to put the gun down and hug her.

He didn't move. In fact he squeezed Lexi's waist even tighter pulling her close to him. She had casted a spell on him so powerful he was willing to kill Pandora rather than give it up. He would protect her at all cost.

"But Kojack, I love you. You were my first—"

"Oh shut the fuck up, Pandora. You're so pathetic! If you wanna get technical bitch I was your first." Lexi snapped smacking her lips.

"I don't give a fuck about being your first. I told you, you should've told me about that shit. You could've still had that shit man. Straight up." Kojack replied.

The bright lights of two cars sprayed across their faces causing them to shield themselves with their hands trying to see who was coming up on them. They parked directly behind the accident and exited their cars one right behind the other. Diamond walked at a faster pace trying to get to Lexi before the man caught up with her. She was too late. He had grabbed her arm just as she was nearing them pulling her back to his side.

"Oh so you do have a twin, huh? I guess you weren't lying." The man spoke tugging on Diamond's arm.

She displayed a disgruntled look on her face trying to tug away but it was no use against the six-foot over two hundred pound man. Pandora gasped noticing that he was the same figure from the parking garage except now she was able to put a face to the silhouette. This was one of those times she wished she had her piece still. Kojack lowered his gun but kept it right by his side.

"You're the bitch that cut Sun up like that and stole his work, huh?" The man spat at Pandora smiling.

"I…no it was her! She's Diamond. She's the one you've been looking for." Pandora snapped pointing to her twin.

"Bitch, I was in the car. You fucked that nigga up, not me." Diamond spat. "Just tell the truth now. You burnt up."

"What?" Kojack exclaimed in disbelief. "It was y'all?"

"Mmhmm." Lexi said curling up her lips then covering her mouth realizing what she had just done.

"Damn, you was there too?" Kojack asked turning to Lexi pushing her away.

"Kojack, I didn't do shit. I left. I told her to come on and she told me to go on. So I did. I didn't know what she was going to do to him. Neither of us did." Lexi rambled pleading her case.

Kojack stepped back shaking his head wondering what the hell he had gotten himself into fucking with these bitches. The man released Diamond's arm chuckling. Everyone looked bewildered at his laughter as Diamond moved from his reach moving around behind Lexi. It was over the jig was up but Pandora was not about to let this nigga shoot her right there at dawn. She refused to go out like that determining that if she were going out it would be with a bang. Pandora looked at everyone's position around the wreck then turned to haul ass back around her car. Just as she reached the site of the wreck the man cocked his gun aiming it dead for her.

"I wouldn't do that just yet." The man yelled after her.

Pandora stopped dead in her tracks backing up slowly hoping she wouldn't turn around to a bullet in her face. Kojack stepped back shielding the ladies behind him. He didn't know what was going down but he prepared, taking his piece off of safety, realizing shit was about to get real. The man glanced over at Kojack raising one eyebrow giving him the 'nigga I wish you would' eye.

"Alright let's all be cool here." The man said reaching around to his back pocket.

He pulled out his cell phone punching it one time as if he had whomever he needed to call on speed dial.

"Yeah, This is Officer Jacobs. I got 'em." He said.

Sirens could be heard from around the corner as cop cars, marked and unmarked, jumped out of nowhere. There was even a paddy wagon that pulled up along the sidewalk all crazy like. Men and women in small bullet proof vests, white tees and jeans hopped out radioing in on the walkie talkies strapped to their chests and talking amongst each other. Some were even high fiving each other on a bust well done with no casualties.

"What the hell is this?" Pandora asked confusingly.

"This is you, under arrest for the brutal murder of Sun Andrews and the distribution of narcotics." Officer Jacobs spat handcuffing Pandora.

"Wait me? What about them?" Pandora shrugged.

The officers glanced over at Kojack still holding his gun but attempting to conceal it. They put their hands on their sides securing their guns just in case he tried any funny business. Kojack slowly got down on his knees knowing the routine from years of watching his boys go through it. He dropped the gun without them even needing to ask then placed his hands on his head interlocking his fingers and rolling his eyes.

Lexi was nervous about her lover going to jail on gun possession and began to cringe at the very thought. She needed that dick like she needed water and wasn't prepared to be without it just yet. She bit her nails nervously hoping they would let him go but wasn't optimistic about it seeing as though they had him down like he was a hardened criminal. It looked like they were hurting him from the facial expressions he was making which pained her even more.

"Don't hurt him motherfucaks! Don't hurt him!" Lexi screamed.

"Ay yo. I gots a license for that in my back pocket." Kojack spat as they detained him searching for evidence of that.

A lady cop took his gun and placed it on the hood of her car while her colleagues continued their investigation. Once they were able to verify his story and everything checked out with Kojack as they helped him to his feet returning his wallet and his gun back him.

Unable to do anything with Kojack the officers focused their attention on Diamond and Lexi asking their Sergeant for a signal to arrest them as well. The dark skinned, bald headed, and buffed Sergeant walked up staring back at the cop placing Pandora in his car then over at Diamond and Lexi.

"Diamond Burden." He said walking up to him lowering his head.

"Why, hello Sergeant Sutters. How are the kids?" She replied in a low seductive voice.

Lexi looked at the two of their faces already knowing what the business was. She knew her sister was a ho but she never knew to what extent. All the business Diamond handled when she got money was strictly her plan and no one else's. Even though Lexi ran with her she never let her in on any of her sexual activities. Those she would have to have gotten on her own.

"They're fine." He replied clearing his throat, in a low voice. "This is why you called me? I can't do anything about this girl."

"Really? Oh gosh, that would be a shame since Mrs. Sutters doesn't know anything about the weekly visits we used to have at the Hilton. Oh and I think this story is going to make national maybe even global news. Isn't it?" She retorted in a babyish voice sucking on her index finger.

He stared down into her devilish puppy dog eyes and knew she wasn't lying about exploiting their love affair. He couldn't afford to let something like that get out especially at the height of his career and especially not since she was fifteen years old at the time of their escapades. Sergeant Sutters folded his buff arms leaning back in a strong firm stance staring down at the short girl wondering if he should call her bluff or not. He scratched his chin, tapping his feet back and forth between each other.

"If your name comes up later in the game that's on you. Alright? But for now just get the fuck outta here. Gone." He said as he walked away pretending as if he had never spoken to them.

Diamond nodded her head in agreement. She didn't want to tell him right then in front of everybody that he should probably get tested, the timing just didn't seem right. She laughed feverishly as she hawked Pandora down. She was heated watching them walk away with Kojack as if they weren't involved in anything. Pandora banged her head repeatedly on the car window pissed at the sight.

"What the fuck? You think you slick you ugly ass tramp? She's a tramp that's why she gets her way! Tramps always get their way! I wouldn't open my legs for every Tom, Dick, and Harry that's why I don't get what I want! Don't worry bitch, I'll be out of here in no time and as soon as I post bail bitch, you're dead! You hear me? Dead!"

Diamond and Lexi looked at each other as the officers drove off. The paddy wagon had two men in the back of it and they were peeking their heads out of the holes in the back doors trying to get a glimpse of them.

It didn't worry Diamond about their significance because whoever they were, they were gone now. Pandora's words rang through Lexi's ears like church bells.

"Diamond, you know we gone have to waste that bitch right?" She spat walking up to Kojack sliding her small arm around his waist.

"Why you say that lil' sis?"

"Cause she's gonna post bail and she's gonna come looking for us." Lexi replied.

"Will she, Lex? Will she?"

Chapter 25- Silly Rabbit

The thick paned sliding glass doors shut like dungeon doors behind Pandora. They booked her and threw her in lockup so quick it made her head spin. She looked around at the filthy room filled with metal bleacher seats and scratched up concrete floors. There was a brick wall on the side of a small dingy toilet in the corner and it looked as if it hadn't been cleaned in centuries and an old beat up pay phone hung on the wall adjacent from it. It was early morning so there were only a few women in the holding cell at that time. She checked out a few areas evaluating a clean place to take a seat as she wondered when the state's attorney would begin releasing bails.

Pandora glanced over at the older black woman sitting a few seats down from her, the young black girl posted directly across from her but she was sleeping under the seat instead of on top of it, and a pregnant middle aged frail white crack head going through withdrawals all the way on the other side of the room. Pandora held her head high, confident that she would be getting out soon. There was no way she was spending a night in that rat infested piss hole.

"Well, what you in for?" The pregnant crack head asked shivering as if it was brick ass in there.

"Who you talking to?" Pandora snapped sucking her teeth.

"Oh, I see we got a feisty one here." The crack head spat laughing. "Well, the old lady beat up a cop for trying to check her insurance. That girl there is waiting on her daddy to come and get her cause she was drinking under aged and I'm a pregnant prostitute dope fiend. So, what the fuck is your story?"

"I ain't got no story."

"Everyone has a story. So tell me yours."

"You know, if we was on the street, I would've sold you your fix with your damn belly sticking out like that and why you ask? Cause I wouldn't give a fuck what your story was. So stop prying into my life trying to figure out mines." Pandora snapped crossing her arms and turning her nose up at her.

The crack head wobbled over to where she was sitting, posted in the seat directly in front of her. Pandora tried to scoot away but the lady kept invading her space not allowing her to get away that easily.

"What?" Pandora snapped staring her dead in the eye.

The lady chuckled unaffected by her macho attitude. "What's your name girly?"

"Ugh, Pandora."

"Pandora, eh? Like the box."

"What? What box?"

"Oh you know, you've heard of the box. Zeus gives this girl the box, tells her not to open it but she opens it anyway." The lady responded.

Pandora didn't have the foggiest idea of what she was talking about. The lady rolled her eyes at how young and dumb she was. She knew she had to have heard of the story since she felt everyone had heard of it.

"The girl opens the box right and it's got all kinds of shit in there, hunger, plague, disease. You name it and it was in that damn box. Well Zeus says don't open it but he doesn't tell her why. So her earth husband opens it and let's the shit out but only let's out a little and closes it but then her dumb ass comes along and opens it letting the rest out." The lady spat picking at her nails.

"What the fuck does that have to do with me?" Pandora spat back.

"Well, I can bet that your story is you've opened that box and tried to close it but all the shit done got out already and now you're fucked."

"Thanks for telling me a whole bunch of nothing." Pandora snarled sarcastically.

"Hmph." The lady said as she moved over to the seat she was in at first. "Don't you wanna know the one thing that didn't come out the box?"

"No. I think I've had enough of your bullshit for one morning. Thanks." Pandora flipped her hair turning her attention to the officers huddled at the window.

She noticed them holding a slew of files, hoping to God one of those were hers. A lady officer opened the door and steeped in looking around at the filth shaking her head. She looked through the files once more before raising her head and calling names. The officer pointed as she called the names of everyone but Pandora's. She was confused as to why she had skipped over her.

"Um, did you forget me?"

"Why would I forget ya?" The officer retorted as she took the other girls then exited the cell.

Pandora put her head down and flopped back down on the seat. The waiting was the worst pain she had ever had. She walked to the end of the holding cell banging on the thick paned glass like she had lost her mind.

"Hey! Hey!" She yelled calling after the pregnant crack head.

She turned back to see what she wanted leery of the fact that the cops would grow impatient. Pandora didn't even have to ask. She had already known what she wanted.

"Hope. There was the spirit of hope left." The lady yelled through the glass as she allowed herself to be hauled away through another set of thick glass doors.

Her words shattered glass in Pandora's head awaking her confidence again. She wasn't about to let this beat her, especially since it was Diamond and Lexi who needed the beating. The sun was done creeping in and was now shining tremendously through the high small square windows at the top of the cell wall.

Pandora couldn't tell what time it was or how much time had elapsed since she was arrested but she felt it wasn't long. She knew they couldn't leave her in there to fester without so much as anything to eat or drink and that they would eventually come for her like they did the others.

****

The sun's rays moved across the floor gradually then slowly made it's way up the side of the other wall when Pandora noticed she had been in there an awfully long time. She had one hell of a headache from hunger and she had to pee badly but refused to use that grotesque thing they portrayed as a commode. Pandora headed over to the pay phone thinking of only one number she could call that might remotely help her out. She dialed the number hoping that her collect call would be accepted.

"You have one free call. You may make it now." The officer said on the line before patching her through to the dial tone.

Oh thank God! She thought as she dialed the number again.

"Hello?"

"Pastor, it's Pandora."

"Yeah. What do you want?" He replied.

"I need for you to come down to 22nd and get me out of here. I don't know why they got me here but I need your help. Can you do that for me?"

"Help? Hmph. That's funny that you call me when you need some help but all I ever asked of you girls was to help me and you see where that got me."

"Pastor, what are you talking about?" She asked bewildered at his rambling.

"Help. That's what I'm talking about. Motherfucking help."

CLICK!

"UGH!!!" Pandora screamed as she slammed the phone against the receiver repeatedly.

"Hey! If you got some money to pay for that then you can break it all you want. Otherwise I suggest you calm it down in there." A female officer said over an intercom.

Pandora plopped down on the bench as more officers brought in their round up for the morning. She scooted to the edge of the last seat leaning on the wall crossing her arms and legs not wanting to touch or talk to anybody. The noise in the cell boggled her brain wishing she could tell them to shut up so badly but the females they had brought in all looked like they had done hard time before. Pandora was in no mood to get her ass whooped.

"Pandora Durden." A female officer called as she opened the door.

"That's Burden and yes that's me."

"Oh excuse me, Pandora Burden." The officer said sarcastically. "Come with me Ms. Burden."

The officer grabbed her by the arm and pulled her to the hallway closing the door behind them. Pandora was elated. She was finally making progress on getting out of that hellhole. They two walked around the corner then down a long hallway in near darkness and silence. The voices of irate caged inmates echoed the place making Pandora a little uneasy but the thought of her release made it all worth wild. They came to a halt at the door at the end. Pandora wiped her hands then locked her fingers behind her back as instructed and spread her legs a little ways apart allowing the officer to check her once more before they entered the room. The officer escorted through the door right up to the counter in the front.

"Alright, now your bail is fifty thousand dollars. Now you know you only need ten percent of that. So if you got five thousand you get to walk until your court date." The cop said popping gum in her face.

"No problem. Can I bail myself out?"

"You sure can. Follow me." The cop led her down to the office where her belongings were being held.

She handed her the bag with all of her stuff as she sifted through looking for her small coach wallet. It was already open when she found it pissing her off a tad bit until she looked through it realizing that the only thing that was missing was $200 in cash. That was to be expected, sucking her lips at their thirsty asses. She pulled out her Chase debit card and handed it to the clerk behind the desk.

The clerk snatched it giving Pandora attitude. Pandora returned the attitude not caring about hers. Shouldn't have brought your ass to work if you didn't want to be here. She thought as she tapped her foot and grabbed the pen out of the cup waiting for the receipt to sign.

BEEP.

The machine beeped rather loud. The clerk leaned in closer to the screen to make sure she was seeing the words correctly. Denied. She swiped it along side of the computer on the card swipe again just in case she may have swiped it too fast the first time. Beep. Denied.

"Um, your card has been denied." The clerk spat handing Pandora her card.

"No, that's not possible. Swipe it again please." Pandora responded daintily.

The clerk snatched it back out of her hand staring her in the face and swiped it not once but three more times. Every time the machine read the same thing. Denied. Denied. Denied.

"Sorry." The clerk said as she whipped the card back towards her way.

Pandora stood there stunned, vexed even as to what was wrong with her card. She didn't panic feeling like it could all be straightened out, easily.

"Could I just use your phone to call the bank? There must be some sort of mistake." Pandora said coyly.

"You've already used your one free call." The cop said standing next to her.

"Please, I'm begging. It will only take a second."

The cop reluctantly nodded her head towards the phone next to the clerk's computer. Pandora could not dial fast enough, punching the numbers profusely keeping the cop's face in sight. She didn't want to piss her off hoping that she would be her one best friend at least until she got out. She zoomed through the prompts knowing them like the back of her hand. Typing her card number in and her pin code was done in a flash. Pandora waited as the automated system ran through her information and verified it. She listened carefully as the computer read her the script it was prompted to:

As of today's date, there are no available funds in this account at this time. If you have any further questions please contact your local bank.

Pandora felt nauseated, sick to her stomach as her headache suddenly worsened and her air was beaten out of her. She had no idea what the hell was going on or who was playing a sick joke on her but it wasn't the least bit funny. It was hard for her to swallow but she knew somehow, someway Diamond and Lexi had something to do with it. Her head became light, as did her feet unable to feel the floor anymore. Her body plummeted to the floor unwillingly, struggling to grab something to save her but it was too late. Pandora hit the floor dazed and seemingly unconscious.

She awoke only a few minutes later remembering exactly the reason why she fell out in the first place. Her thoughts were distraught, feeling like she was doomed,

9 780615 693095

never to get out of the shitty ass place which the state would deem her home for only God knew how long. With all the cops posted around her trying to revive her, she grabbed one of the guns out of the holster of a nearby cop and pointed it to her head. The team of cops worked to restrain her, grabbing her arms and legs to hold her down but for a little thing she was very strong. She quickly shoved the gun back against her temple, closed her eyes then pulled the trigger.

STAY UP TO DATE O

WITH

FOLl

Fc

@NICE

LIKE ME (

.com/NIC

DON'T FOR(

#GET

#VISUA

#TEA

CPSIA information can b
Printed in the USA
LVOW06s2205201013

357807LV0001